Also by Matthew Rettenmund
ENCYCLOPEDIA MADONNICA

BOY CULTURE

MATTHEW RETTENMUND

ST. MARTIN'S PRESS ≈ NEW YORK

BOY
CULTURE
MATTHEW
RETTENMUND

This novel is a work of fiction. All of the
events, characters, names, and places depicted
in this novel are entirely fictitious or are
used fictitiously. No representation that any
statement made in this novel is true or that
any incident depicted in this novel actually
occurred is intended or should be inferred by
the reader.

Editor: Ensley Eikenburg
Production Editor: Lisa Vecchione
Copyedited by Pamela Loeser
Design by Junie Lee

Library of Congress Cataloging-in-Publication Data

Rettenmund, Matthew.
    Boy culture / Matthew Rettenmund.
        p.   cm.
    ISBN 0-312-14553-5
    1. Gay men—United States—Fiction. 2. Male
prostitution—United States—Fiction. I. Title.
PS3568.E774B68 1995
813'.54—dc20   95-22172
                                         CIP

10 9

For, of course, *Mom.*

Special thanks in no particular order to:
JJ, a wunderkind
Melissa, a goddess
Zafar, a sister
Sandra, a coconspirator
Tim, a gal-pal
Lori, a catch
Rebecca and Mark, critics
Matthew, a partyboy
Jane, a teacher
Danielle, a cheerleader
Ensley, a Henry Higgins
and
Ron, who's forgotten me by now; the best
fuck I ever had.

"To be homosexual is to be a
natural-born liar. To actually *be*
gay is to tell the truth. Cross my
heart."
—some haggard old queen, 1995

INTRODUCTION: NOW

Why are gay guys obsessed with storytelling? Why do they ruin all sense of romance by asking, on the first date, "What was your first time like? What was your best time like? What was your last time like?" Why do they care?

The men I slept with used to ask me all of the above and more, sometimes requiring me to tell stories about sex *while* we were actually *having sex*. I think that they were still hungry for talk about being gay from all those pent-up years as kids. As children, they spent their existences craning their necks and opening their ears for absolutely *any* reference to the thing that compelled them to watch the man next door mow the lawn . . . without his shirt . . . *sweating*. When they started sleeping with other men (or with the man next door), they were so excited to get more information on the subject that it became a fetish, something they would require from every man they'd ever meet.

Of course, I'm no better. I may lack the sort of dating experience of the average gay man, but I'm observant enough to know that these things go on, and that I've been deprived of my chance to ask questions and tell stories.

So, now that I've got your ear, I'm going to tell you the story I've always wanted to tell, along with any other small tale that comes up along the way. I'm . . . *venting*.

Let's get a few things straight right off the bat:

• This story, *my* story, is a confession. Lucky for you, confessions are the *hottest* of all stories. Ask any priest. And considering the sexualities of most of the principal players in my story, the priest reference is doubly appropriate.

• I'm not Catholic, but from what I understand, confessions can also be painful. After all, the guy confessing is telling a story he feels he *has* to tell just to get over it. If that's true, then this confession is no exception.

• There is not necessarily a moral in a confession. In fact, people confess precisely because they know their behavior is in conflict with some understood moral. So you won't be finding any obnoxious lessons at the end of this story. Instead, you can deconstruct the story and figure out what, if any, lessons there are to be learned. Or you can flip to the dirty parts and jerk off. Be my guest. I'd probably do the latter if I were you.

• And lastly, confessions are anonymous. You won't catch me breaking any of the rules of the genre.

Call me "X."

PROLOGUE: RECENTLY

Norman is a pediatrician. I believe he intentionally chose that occupation to make his life a series of progressively narrowing closets. He's lived for twenty-five years above his small neighborhood practice—he's probably treated every young parent and all their children in the whole community, girls and boys alike. If anyone knew he loved sex with men, his business would fall like primary teeth out of a kid's face, the nonsensical equation being that gay equals child molester.

"Daddy," he said evenly, as soon as I'd closed the door of our hotel room. It's preposterous, really—I'm half his age.

Norman half sat against the back of a sofa situated in the middle of the room. As I adjusted myself to the stiffly clean space and took an Evian from the refrigerator, I endured his wordless stare.

Norman started rubbing his chest through the short-sleeved dress shirt he wore, trying to be sexy for me, as if my being horny mattered at all. I, in response, shifted and deliberately looked hot and bothered. I watched the middle-aged man who was going slightly to fat and gray (think: Ned Beatty). I eyed him as a pedophile might eye a fresh young boy, a look I can pull from an invisible bag of tricks without having any firsthand experience.

Norman loosened his slacks, let them slip off—he was naked underneath, a still-young-looking hard-on stiff against his soft belly.

He was never completely relaxed on our dates, but his own discomfort was, I suppose, a large part of the turn-on for Norman.

He turned around and bent over the sofa, his ass broad and pale but relatively inoffensive. Any number of bored housewives would probably giggle with glee over an ass like Norman's, but I wasn't a bored housewife—I was a bored call boy.

Norman's ass wasn't my first choice right then, wouldn't have been under any circumstances. That fact reminded me of margarine, of how you'll eat it in a pinch if there's no real butter around. It's funny, the things you'll think of when you're gearing up to fuck.

Norman didn't talk much, didn't need me to call him "boy," though I would have if he'd asked. I don't think he'd have been able to handle the implications of his Daddy/boy fantasy if I'd reciprocated. My calling him "boy" could have led to him saying something else, something more explicit. It might have unsettled him enough to make him guilty while examining his actual-boy clients. He probably already had an ulcer over seeing a prostitute; who knows what living out a vaguely pedophilic fantasy would do to him?

I took my time getting to him—the anticipation is what he savored most, I think. He could hear me undoing my belt, sliding it through the loops of my jeans, letting it drop with a thud-clink. I unbuttoned my jeans, unzipped, tugged them down to my ankles. Norman was shifting around, straining to hear every noise I made.

I stepped out of my jeans and padded across the too new carpet toward the bull's-eye.

Norman liked me more than any other man he'd been with. Why? I'm cute enough, I suppose. I'm average height, broad-shouldered and solid without being all that well built. My hair is brown with a touch of blond here and there where either the sun or misguided dollops of Oxy 10 have stripped bits of the pigment away. I'm fit, I'm young, I'm standing around with my erection tent-poling my underwear—what's not to like?

I'm no prize pig, but for Norman, and for all the Normans I'd fucked before, I was the Perfect Man because I was *there*. And I was willing.

I walked over to Norman and nestled my groin—still safe behind thin Jockeys—into the moist split of his ass. I bumped into him softly, bracing myself with the flats of my palms against his slick back.

I knew Norman very well. I knew I would stick my finger in my mouth, slip the finger into his asshole, finger-fuck him while his gasps communicated that it made him feel really good. At last, when he started panting, almost like strangulated speech, when his cock was raw from humping the sofa, I would tug my dick out, glove it with the spare I kept in a pouch in the elastic of my shorts, and give it to him fast and hard, the way he wanted it. No lube except for the stuff that came with the rubber. Not 100 percent safe, but damn close since Norman didn't require *me* to get off and he'd tested negative every six months for the previous ten years.

To keep it up as I fucked the hell out of Norman, I thought of erotic things—a man's underarm, men in sweatpants, Hart Bochner. It's often necessary to get off by prox. I was screwing, but wishing *I* were getting screwed; Norman was getting screwed, but wishing he were twelve years old, an entirely different person. Neither one of us really wanted to be with the other. We *had* to be.

Margarine.

Still, for an old guy, Norman retained a square jaw, and he really knew how to get fucked, which is surely an underrated talent. I've even lost it while doing it to him, which surprised me both times it happened, even though by then I already knew things were changing for me. By then, I had someone more realistic than Hart Bochner to fantasize about when I closed my eyes, someone so hot that just thinking of him screwing me could make me come while screwing a man older than my father.

Later, after my meticulous shower and Norman's traditional pack and a half of cigarettes, he chatted for about five minutes about the weather, his day at work, my performance, blah-blah-blah. I tugged my jeans on and brought up the possibility of my retiring. He cut me off before I could explain.

Looking completely crestfallen from within his fluffy white robe, all bundled up and yet still insecure, Norman pouted, "I hope you'll change your mind. I'll miss it a great deal."

I smiled and avoided his gaze, searching for my shoes. He'll miss *it*, but I'll bet he won't miss *me*. "Don't worry, Norman," I said soothingly, "I think I still have a few tricks left up my sleeve." *Wink*.

Norman tightened the sash on his robe reflexively. I could see he was searching for the tone that would persuade me to keep on working. It would be the same doctorly tone he used to persuade children that shots are not, in fact, painful.

"No, really. You're the best. You're too young to stop yet." He gently cupped the bulge in my jeans as if it were sacred. "You know me too well . . . No one else will bother to figure out my exact needs."

He was probably right. The other boys he'd end up with would probably do only what they absolutely had to, and not very well at that. I pulled away casually and pulled on my tennis shoes, leaving them unlaced. "You're sweet, Norman." Case closed.

I'd tell him more about my retirement plan later, over the phone.

Norman is one of the tender-hearts, an inflated, aging child who speaks so plaintively and with such feeling, it embarrasses. He does not molest children. I believe that because he told me when I'd quizzed him on it, and no man on earth can lie to me. In his fantasy, Norman isn't the older man getting his jollies from screwing a little boy, he's the little boy who—impossibly—*loves every minute of it*. Fantasies never make sense.

So, yes I *do* feel that kids are safe around Norman. *Especially* little boys, in whose welfare he has a special and empathetic interest. After all, he's one of them.

Maybe that's why I feel drawn to him, even now, as phase one of my brilliant career draws to a close.

I hope you paid attention. This is one of those *Old Yeller*–type beginnings.

THE CONFESSIONS: THEN

I AM

A

WANNA-BE

The beginning of the end occurred a while before the events of this story. I was riding the Jeffery #6 bus from Hyde Park to Michigan Avenue, sitting about ten seats behind and to the left of this really cute guy, closely monitoring his bodily activities. He kept flicking his hair (nervous) and chewing at his nearly nonexistent nails (nervous), and also kept bobbing his left knee in the aisle in large, quick jerks (nervous and a little . . . excited? About what?). He was *so* hot, definitely stalkable.

I recognized him from a senior-year class of mine. He looked *different,* though not necessarily *better.* And yet I hadn't found him remotely arousing years earlier, when I'd had a legitimate excuse to talk to him. We'd never spoken, but I'd heard a lot about him.

I questioned my sanity. Why should I spend my time stalking a ridiculous college kid with nervous tics? Why should I stalk anybody? I deserved a stalker of my own.

The bus swerved to avoid a pedestrian strolling across the street toward the clearly illuminated DON'T WALK sign, jolting me from my boy-reverie. I became aware of a wailing police siren and caught the alternating red glow on the windows. Everyone was watching intently the scene just ahead: a pair of economy autos crunched up like baby accordions, a hysterical ambulance, and several police cars. The bus kept going after it had carefully maneuvered around the scene, and nobody cared to turn around and watch anymore.

Except for Nervous, who arched his neck and looked straight back at the deserted catastrophe, eyes still plaintively searching for casualties. Then he glanced slightly to his left and right into my probably rude-seeming stare.

I can't believe this really happened myself, but I *looked away*. I haven't looked away from a guy's stare since kindergarten, and indeed can go for hours without blinking, and now that it really counted, I choked.

My big chance to get the point across to this cute kid that I wanted to have his baby, and I blew it. My retinas carried a red image of what he'd looked like in the moment of visual contact: blond and sleek, cheekbones that gave you a nosebleed just looking at them, red lips.

This is not the story of how I fell in love with a college kid and lived happily ever after. *Please!* Wanting to have his baby translated into *He's kind of cute, and sex with him might actually be fun for a change.*

Dating? I'd never. Oh, sure, I'd had men take me out to dinner, but it was always to kill time between fuckings.

Schoolboy crushes happen every day. I'm not saying I'm unique for having one, but I *am* saying that for me, this was a watershed moment.

I made money the old-fashioned way—I fucked for it. There's nothing wrong with that and I never had a moral dilemma over it. It was an easy way to thrive. But if the act was easy to perform, the rest had been trickier. In all my years as a call boy, I'd never had a personal life on the side. I didn't have sex for pleasure, didn't get incredibly turned on by other guys, didn't fall in love. Fall in love! It was like my sex drive was in limbo, much less my love drive.

But that day on the bus was a revelation. I was sitting there drooling over a sexy boy just like any normal gay guy would, just as if I'd been able to all along. But I hadn't. But I was.

Seriously considering a college kid as my reintroduction to pleasure-sex was a little absurd, though. I had graduated from the degree factory a few short years previously, but my work kept me running around near campus, lots of lonely bachelor professors. I probably spent more time near the campus two years after I graduated than I did when I was attending classes. I felt like those poor souls who, after thirteen years of detention, chastisement, and being held back in the sixth grade twice, finally graduate high school, but for some reason keep hanging around the building. They're free to go, but something keeps bringing them back. Toward the end, high school life has become too familiar and *easy* for them to just walk away from it. I guess that's why I was investing my first sexual interest since the eighties in a college kid. If college taught me anything at all, it was that college kids are *easy*.

Nervous wore a Blondie T-shirt. *Blondie!* So retro. It had been ten years since anyone had heard of Blondie-the-band, and the lead singer (whom everyone called "Blondie," anyway) had been off-and-on, doing the disco diva thing. And yet here was a brilliant kid at a first-rate school somewhere in the Midwest wearing a Blondie concert T-shirt.

There had been a rumor on the gay grapevine that his room itself was blond, blond, blond, antique posters of the band stretched across every surface. He supposedly had a pair of undies autographed by her, too, and one wall entirely made up of a single, crazily blown-up photograph, barely discernible, of a sweaty, grinning Nervous hugging a sweaty, woozy Blondie, a quickie photo snatched after a New York performance when Nervous was way too young to have been allowed into any club, guaranteeing he'd be first in line at the stage door.

I was almost caught up in that sort of narcotic obsession once—just one time. I was in a chain record store, killing time on a shopping spree. I hate chains and never find stuff I want in those places—everything priced "TJ" and "TG" and "TF," not "11.99," "12.99," "6.99—SALE." All the categories are broad, with few real choices, arranged systematically in a warehouselike room. I was browsing by the cutouts—*albums,* that is, LPs, VINYL. The real thing. Scratch 'n nick, pop and whir, round and round.

There was a mass of music lovers mulling about the warehouse, chattering noisily over Softcell's "Tainted Love," CD-crystal-clear, pumped through invisible speakers. The song was dated, the enjoyability timeless. It took me back to the eighth grade and an odd, euphoric little feeling of "oh-my-God-I'm-gay-and-will-never-be-free-and-must-run-away-to-find-love," a complete flashback triggered by the music. Someone was standing off to my left, arms folded, staring directly at me, a bold presence that stood unmoving while I was thumping back to the eighties with Softcell, flipping past horribly useless albums whose existence was a joke—Haircut 100, Breakfast Club, *Kajagoogoo.* I almost resisted confronting the starer, still influenced by the trance that I was thirteen and couldn't dare to "look" because someone may "see." Always the fixation on sight.

Then I snapped out of it and turned with all the confidence and questioning of a man, a homosexual, and a whore.

It was a life-sized cardboard stand-up display of Madonna, white skin, red dress, black fishnets. BOOM—the nineties.

The stand-up was a piece of work, assembled from three separate parts, legs-torso-head. Madonna's hair was Marilyn-white, no roots visible, obscured by several washes of bleach and photographic wizardry. It was shoulder-length, medium curly, halfway between "Breathless Mahoney" and *Desperately Seeking Susan.* The eyes were slits, jet-black lashes, ivory lids, arched brows allowed to grow wild around the edges. Her lips, cruelly pointed, were scratched onto the mannish face and smeared burgundy, tiny-gapped front teeth just discernible between. The gown was a clinging red nightmare running down her sleek body, adhering to and softening angular hips, exposing 90 percent of the trademark bosom and falling just far enough left of center to cover all signs of pubes while still leaving the left leg exposed. The leg sported large-holed black fishnets, snagged intentionally, artistically, at the knee.

I loved that stand-up. I have always snapped my fingers to Madonna's music, and I enjoy her cunty attitude as an antidote to all the butt-kissing celebs who gush thanks to God on high. And let's face it: Madonna could do a credible infomercial for prostitution. I had good reasons to like The Big M. Even so, no star had ever attracted more than my passing appreciation.

But this stand-up *changed* me.

All the elements I've described were nothing without her facial expression. It was rapturous, showy, realistic, calculated, spontaneous, angry, elated surrender captured on film, propped up promotionally probably two in each mall all over the planet.

Who could ever make that particular face except Madonna, and yet how surprising for me to find such a gem of an expression in such a common source, like discovering a Mona Lisa smile on the face of a milk-carton child.

I stared at her for a minute, my gaze traveling down the cardboard, with its impression of sumptuous folds of material. I followed the curve of her breasts and stared at the space between them, trying to enter her soul via the unseen left nipple.

For that moment, I felt absorbed into Madonna, feeling how she'd felt posing for that picture: *depressed at having recently lost a friend, excited at impending critical acclaim, fear of failure forever providing the bass, horniness and no time to screw until May—and the joy of being fabulously famous.*

In that moment of utter surrender to adulation, to desiring perfect, vicarious, romantic deification, I understood what it is to be a gay man. It's all about intensity.

That's why it was possible for me to go for ten years without desiring another man and *still* identify myself as gay. My gayness isn't about sex, even though my prostitution was.

I carefully tucked away my unguarded reaction before continuing to shop for records.

I got the assistant manager to sell me Madonna for seventy-five dollars cash-and-carry and a promise to keep quiet about it. The time and the pose are past, but the stand-up lives on in my walk-in closet. I take my cue from that thing.

It sits in my otherwise empty closet with a flattering overhead light, sporting a crucifix I got from one of my priest-clients. Even though my roommate Joe was probably a bigger Madonna fan than Madonna is, I never told him about my stand-up. He mentioned once that he was trying to get one from various collectors' services for as mercifully close to two hundred dollars as possible.

No doubt about it, Nervous was making me shake with lust. What did I do about it? Not a thing. Why should I? Like I said, this was a first for me. I wanted to ease into the idea. There was no sense in losing my virginity all over again to the first guy to turn my head. Instead, I decided to be happy that I was functional again, and to bide my time, look for a guy I both lusted after and flipped for.

I didn't stop and think, *Why is this happening now? What is motivating me?* If I had, I might have realized there was no motivation at all, just a reaction. I was a frozen nomad, and Nervous was the first bit of heat that would gradually thaw me into a new world. Would I be dead, perfectly preserved meat? Or would I be what Walt Disney hoped to be: miraculously spared from oblivion years after initial death?

I pumped the overhead button to signal the driver, got off the halted bus *(Good-bye, Nervous! Alas, it was never meant to be; I'm no good for you . . .)*, and walked the final two blocks to my apartment.

I knew I was no good for Nervous, but for the first time since Culture Club, I was hungry for something more than just a steady job.

I HAVE
A HEART
OF GOLD

CONFESSION 2

Over a year later, I was still looking for Mr. Right, more determined than ever not to settle for Mr. Right on My Face.

Problem: I knew only two people personally in my apartment building. I wanted to screw one, and the other wanted to screw me. Sex is really *so* unattractive. It's all so ugly, I can hardly discuss it. But in the spirit of the confession, it's about time I shoveled some dirt.

There's Andrew, and I wanted him, and there's Joe, and he wanted me. At least Andrew didn't want Joe, though that particular nightmare haunted me more than one sleepless night.

Andrew and Joe were my roommates. Andrew paid only three hundred dollars of the twelve-hundred-dollar rent (call me generous) and needed time to consider his sexuality (???). I would tell him to be original, avoid the sexual confusion cliché. Everybody's doing that one. He'd just grin and say in Minnesota farm boy, "And being gay is unique or somethin'?" God, I *melt* when a man challenges my authority. Nobody ever did that! If more guys had, I'd have been humbler and probably a lot happier than I was fixating on Andrew.

Joe, on the other hand, was just so *nice*. He worshiped me from anear, a seventeen-year-old who decided I looked like his first lover. At first I paid little attention to the friendly kiddo I had allowed to live with me after his older brother/guardian had approved it. Joe's parents had disowned him; he'd been loudly gay since he was thirteen, and his brother—a sexy straight schnook named Tony—was attempting to be progressive, figuring that Joe's living with a nice-seeming boy like me was better than life on the streets. Tony never realized I *was* the streets.

Eventually I enjoyed chatting with Joe, his moppish blond hair reminiscent of a cute shaggy dog's. I must have blocked it out when he would say, "Hi!" and make it sound like *Hi?* the unspoken question something like *Are you interested in me yet?*

I was returning from a date at three A.M. the night I first figured out that Joe was after me. By that point in time, I had spotted lots of men I was attracted to (including Joe), but none I would consider a potential Mr. Right (including Joe). None except Andrew.

I sleepily navigated the long, narrow hall of the prudently carpeted second floor toward my familiar door, distracted at the thought of how happily overpaid I was. Joe's room was a small studio in and of itself, directly across from the two-bedroom Andrew and I shared, though Joe always had access to the whole place if he wanted it. You can do that in Chicago: live cheaply on an entire floor of a building.

Just as I got to my door, I heard a soft rustle behind me.

"Hey there," Joe whispered playfully. Then, in the same tone as the *Do you know where your children are?* commercial, "Do you know what time it is?"

I cringed inwardly and turned to face my inquisitor. Joe—despite having one of those ruddy, suburban faces—was a knock-out. He was my height with the graceful, artistically muscled build of a ballet dancer (which he was not) and huge blue eyes about as cunning as Barbie's. That mop of hair I usually associated with him was out of sight, brown with wet and slicked back, and a paper-thin blue shortie robe was apparently all that shielded his nudity from me. Actually, the robe wasn't very thorough in its task, leaving much of his upper body exposed. I remember thinking, *If you're going to bother wearing a robe, why not wear all of it?* just before I put two and two together.

That's how oblivious I was. Until that moment, when I suddenly saw Joe staring at me hopefully, half-naked and *Is that liquor I smell?* tipsy, I had never suspected he was interested in me beyond conversation. But here he was in the middle of the night, stepping out of his closet and letting me know I was a wanted man. I had the perverse thought that he'd been waiting for me at his peephole sipping a bottle of wine and splashing himself at intervals from a bowl of water so as to appear recently showered. That way, he could emerge fresh as a daisy with a "you-caught-me" air about his near-nudity, and do everything short of begging to get me inside and on top.

He was so young, so screwed-up about what he wanted in life, but he was neither too young nor too confused to be anything less than lusty. The physical attraction on my part had been there from the start, if simmering on a back burner. But I was too wise at twenty-five—or so I thought—and the attraction was too wan.

What to do when a naked seventeen-year-old serves himself up to you on a silver platter? Life is so . . . *hard* [said with heart-wrenching agony]. Well, maybe I was overreacting. There was little chance that someone as good-hearted as Joe would be so *manipulative* as to seduce anyone. So *smart*. Joe was a naïve little party animal, a natural slut who loved sex for the fun of it. On the other hand, he could conceivably have planned the charade quite innocently, out of romantic fervor, not wanting to trap me, just wanting to "make love." The unbearable lightness of being Joe.

"I certainly do know what time it is," I yawned. My game was to sound weary enough to discourage him. "What are you doing up so late . . . drinking?"

He was hugging the door's frame, allowing a bare leg to peek out at me, an obscene attempt at coquettishness. Why do I get a sinking feeling when men get all *girlie* on me? Am I homophobic?

"I don't like to drink very much. I mean, I don't very much like to drink, but when I drink, I drink . . . very much!" He laughed and blushed at his tongue twister and shifted to a more natural stance. He looked so pretty just then, so unaffected. Looking unaffected is about as common among gay guys as looking sultry is among nuns. But I don't favor sultry nuns, and I just didn't feel much of an urge for Joe, either. Ultimately he was too "cute" and too "nice." Or so I thought.

I smiled pleasantly and said, "G'night," starting away as if nothing had ever happened.

"Wait a minute," he said quickly, laughing shortly. "Why don't you come in and help me finish the bottle . . . There's only one glass left and I'm saving it for you."

I went against all reason and accepted. Despite my common sense and irascible nature, I am often persuaded to do nice things for nice people. As I crossed the threshold I wondered if I was going to fuck Joe just because he deserved it. That sounds pretty condescending, but I can only speak from the pedestal he'd put me on. If I'd consented and we'd had sex, to me it would have been a fuck between friends, but to him it would have been the lovemaking he'd wanted for ages. Sex can be completely different things to the participants involved, but the one who invests the most in it is the one who determines what it ultimately becomes. Why should I be cruel enough to deny someone happiness when it would be so easy for me to grant it? But that's the catch. It would be absolutely *nothing* to me and absolutely *everything* to him, and eventually I would leave him devastated just as easily as I'd given him pleasure. The power of sex.

I don't have a good working relationship with the power of sex. I have had to deal with disproportionate attraction all my life. High school was one long exercise in unrequited attraction. I would spy a guy with some particularly enticing feature (legs so effortlessly powerful they floored me, a hairy thigh in summer shorts exposed accidentally, a shitty grin) and would go on for weeks trying to convince myself he wanted me, too. And the *girls* who liked *me!* Many of them had dated the studs in our class, but seemed to like me if I made them laugh or carried on a conversation with them. Maybe I should have become a sense-of-humor call boy, or marketed my "We talked for *hours!*" skills.

One of my best high school buddies was a girl. Marie. She was so pretty, but not your typical high school bombshell. Her style was her own, always wearing headbands and jeans and ironed-straight hair and no makeup when the rest of the girls were accessorizing themselves to death, drowning in goo. She had striking features that looked all the more striking up close, which is where she usually was in relation to me. We were pretty inseparable. We *created* the yearbook—a fucking piece of art. And we almost slept together once, huddled together in my room listening to Duran Duran and laughing about how *dumb* the rest of our hometown was. She just suddenly kissed me on the cheek and giggled and apologized, then watched my expression for a red or green light.

I felt bloodless. "I'm . . . gay, Marie," was all I could choke out, and we burst into uncontrollable giggles. She believed me, all right. And she supported me, *et cetera*. But for some reason, we both just laughed our asses off, laughter so unrestrained, it bordered on delirium. Still, there was a part of her smile I never saw again, not because I was gay and therefore weird or amoral, but because I was gay and therefore unattainable. She couldn't do anything about it. She couldn't make me straight. She couldn't turn into a man herself to share that part of me. And no matter how much I tried to continue being her buddy, I couldn't help trying to respond to her subtle, wishful signals, as if trying to make her feel better in her defeat.

I not only disliked being in that no-win position, I despised it. I hated it so much that I dropped Marie like a hot potato. That was my way of convincing myself that I was more powerful than the power of sex.

Joe's bedroom was small. He wasn't supertidy, with wall-to-wall pillows and stacks of disco CDs. The earnestly displayed posters he had chosen for his walls were so popular, they had ceased to have meaning for me, the most familiar Harings and Mapplethorpes available, as common as picking your nose. SILENCE = DEATH stickers glared from the wall around the window, surrounding an elaborate shrine to Madonna that consisted of an old star-shaped poster of her, a candle, an antique crucifix, and dozens of colorful postcards. Scattered on the floor were an elaborate prop magic wand (Joe, the Radical Faerie?), an array of sexy club clothes with unforgiving zippers, and an aromatic urn, an ode to vegetarianism that contained a dozen or more baby herbs. Joe was a vegetarian not for his health or as a statement for animal rights, but because Madonna was one.

The lights were dimmed and on his makeshift milk-crate table was a bottle of wine on a lace tablecloth inherited, he later told me, from the same uncle who had introduced him to sodomy. I understood that this eager setting was for *me*. I'd been all wrong. This was, after all, what they call a Seduction.

"Sit down over there," he said, gesturing toward the larger of the room's two chairs. "You can turn on the fake fire, too. It's freezing in this place."

The fake fire was already plugged in.

"Nice brick," I said of the (fake) brickwork Joe had recently glued around the (fake) fireplace, squirming on the unyielding (but genuine cherrywood—how'd that happen?) chair. "We don't have anything like it across the hall."

Joe sat across from me on the floor, handing up a glass of wine while taking a slug from his own glass. "Well, it helps make this place feel more like home, you know?" He crossed his legs awkwardly and I was grateful for the shadows that obscured what must surely lie within that darkness beyond his robe and between his legs. I'm not sure he knew he was potentially flashing me.

There was a newly added picture of a young guy on the far wall who my failing eyes told me was at least good-looking. "Is that an old picture of Tony?" I squinted.

The mood swung low. Joe practically sank into the carpet and disappeared. He took about two minutes to answer, and in that time I had the perverse pleasure of knowing I had asked exactly the wrong question.

"No," he replied, eyes almost crossing with agony. "No. That's not my brother. That's . . . my . . . first . . . lover . . ." It says something when a seventeen-year-old kid is able to speak of his first lover with a legitimate sense of pathos and reminiscence.

It reminded me of my first serious conversation with Joe, when he'd been so down in the dumps.

"I feel trapped," he'd told me then. "I have no school, no real job, no family to speak of, or who'll talk to me, anyways . . . I want . . . *so much* . . ."

"What do you want?" I urged.

I could feel the ambition surging in Joe's chest as he struggled to articulate his dreams. "I want to be really happy," he said right away. "I want to invent T-shirts that everyone in the country knows about. I want to go to the hottest club in the world and see dozens of my bracelets hanging on the coolest people. I want to make enough money so I won't need anyone to support me, enough that my family will wish they'd never lost me. And I want a really, really strong man to love me and respect me and think my designs are beautiful. You know, all the usual junk. I want to be famous, but I want it to just happen to me instead of killing myself trying to make it happen . . . Oh, what's the use?" He'd gone from elated to defeated in a space of seconds, having successfully tricked himself into believing his dreams had come true, sinking when reality intruded.

"I feel old," Joe sighed, too young to remember "Josie and the Pussycats."

"You can't be old," I snapped. "You're *several* years younger than *me.*" Ouch! The big, bad scorpion had accidentally stung himself.

"I just feel like I've slept around and slept around and *still* can't find a boyfriend. I'm too dumb for college. Look at my job— I'm just unskilled labor." As of that week, he worked, off the books, as a waiter at a restaurant playfully called Jailbait and routinely brought home more money in tips than I could make if I ever decided to sell my butt. "How will I ever keep this up? How can I expect to go anywhere, to be famous and rich, if I'm not even *doing* anything?"

What is this syndrome? Why do so many young gay men feel forty at seventeen? I did myself, except I felt forty at ten. Now, at twenty-six, I still feel forty and *look* twenty-six, which is even scarier. But back to this "washed-up syndrome." It's like a turning point when we feel we've suddenly lived the best, most carefree, years of our lives. Things that precipitate this syndrome include, but are not limited to:

(1) Loss of virginity. Ow! *Oooh!* Bang—you're an adult, not overnight but within five lusty minutes. The instant you come in front of someone, you feel yourself aging. It's usually mistaken for welcome maturation, but in retrospect, you'll be able to identify this moment as a giant leap toward middle age.

(2) Job straight outta hell. The first job you screw up or at which you're doomed by a lousy, petty, self-involved boss, or that you otherwise are dismissed/forced from, or that you are damned to return to forever and a day. All the time you've spent at this job might as well be flushed down the toilet, and no matter when you look at the calendar, you realize you've been there ten times longer than you'd thought. You have, in fact, spent *years* at the job, spinning your wheels while aging . . . aging . . . aging.

(3) First STD. Once you've had crabs, you realize the inherent squalor in sexual activity, and your depression over your newfound contempt for sex makes you realize you *live* for sex. Not to mention if you're lucky enough to get an incurable disease like warts; an incurable and extremely uncomfortable disease like herpes; or an incurable, extremely uncomfortable, and fatal disease like AIDS. All of these diseases, whether as relatively harmless as warts or as unspeakably horrific as AIDS, make you accept that your body—upon its introduction to this new, eternal virus—is changed *forever,* a concept that'll put a good ten years on you in a bad ten seconds flat.

(4) Lovelessness. Self-explanatory, except it bears mentioning that going to your traditional haunts loverless only to find that you've slept with one third of the patrons can be an especially jarring and aging experience.

Joe had probably encountered two or three of these situations in recent times, the virginity thing being the only impossible one since he'd lost his in the Precambrian era. I felt for him, and I thought that to make him feel better, I should feel him up. He'd feel much better very soon, and younger and less useless . . . if only for an hour or so. But isn't that always the way? What do you think sleeping around is all about anyway?

I was touched by Joe. Continually, helplessly touched. He was so sweet, so genuine. Naïve? Maybe. What fag doesn't want to be rich and famous and nyah-nyah to you, you rotten, deserting family? But even I, at my most jaded, could not resist Joe's wishful nature. I longed for that in myself. Being closer to him, maybe I could absorb some . . .

I decided that I knew better than to spoil it by fucking him.

But there in his room, Joe was looking at me with the mooniest eyes I'd ever seen, murmuring that I resembled his first lover.

"Oh," I stammered.

"Chuck."

"Oh."

"He looks just like you." He looked up at me earnestly, trying so hard to catch my attention in just the right way to make me want him. He was so far out on a limb, he was either going to fly or fall, and it was all up to me. I was Mr. Gravity and I got to decide. Decisions, decisions.

"Oh, really?" Smile. "I can't tell from here—I'm too far away."

He rocked toward me, sitting up on his knees with either hand on either side of me on the couch.

"Well . . . I'm close enough to tell. And you're a dead ringer."

Joe knew I was a prostitute. He'd known from day one, when I was moving some of my stuff around to accommodate his stuff and my little black book landed at his feet.

"Gee whiz," he'd said sarcastically. "This is the biggest black book I've ever seen."

"Yeah, well, you know what they say about the black ones being bigger," I teased, snatching it away.

"You'd about have to be a *hustler* to fill a black book that size."

I'd set down my load, stared him defiantly in the eye, and said, "Actually, I *am.*"

He'd been about to speak, but shut up on seeing my unwavering glare. Instead of being creeped out, he'd finally shrugged, smiled, and said, *"Cool."*

I should've known *then* the trouble I'd be in later, in the apartment, late at night, with Joe throwing himself at, around, and over me.

The smell of soap and Joe's skin was almost intoxicating enough to convince me to give in after all. *Who knows? Maybe I'll like it.* But something was wrong. I couldn't have gotten an erection if I'd tried. It's easy when you're being paid, not so easy when it's on your own dime. Or maybe it was that I actually liked Joe and didn't want to screw him up worse than he already was.

There was *something* wrong, all right: *He's just not Andrew.*

"Hey, kiddo, you're too close for comfort," I said gently, and tousled his damp hair. *If only I could blow-dry it and bring that mop back.*

He sat back down instantly, smiling a hollow, little-boy smile. "I'm sorry. I just . . ."

"No, don't be. It's just . . . you know. I don't like to fuck nonclients lately. I'd almost feel . . . *unfaithful . . .*" I was floundering, but Joe *did* know I hadn't been involved with anyone since he'd known me. He bought it.

Joe laughed amiably. "No, no, I understand. Being faithful is cool . . . I wish my first boyfriend had *been* like you instead of *looking* like you. You know, when I found out how many other guys he'd been with while we were together, it almost turned me straight."

"Two wrongs don't make a right," I quipped. "I guess I'm a workaholic. I'm also dead-tired. I can't finish my wine, I'm afraid." I gingerly placed the glass in his hands and stood to leave. He followed me to the door bouncily, trying to distract attention from the fact that he'd just been shot down, chattering rapidly. I squeezed his arm to show no harm done and took off, slinking across the hall to my room.

I AM
A SLAVE
TO MY
SEX DRIVE

Joe took too much notice of me, but if Andrew had ever given me so much as a sidelong glance, I'd definitely have been at a loss for innuendo.

I stepped into my apartment and closed my door to all thoughts of Joe's innocent desire, allowing the darkness inside the place to envelop me.

It was shattered by Andrew's question.

"Where were *you*?"

I shivered, my arm stretching across the wall at my side, fingers groping to twist the lights on. Hazy light crept in as I turned the knob, brighter and brighter until I could see the dull flesh tones of Andrew's chest, the shine of his eyes and cheeks. No teeth—*uh-oh*, not smiling? Impossible. But my adjusting eyes verified the suspicion.

I sensed that bright lights would be unwelcome. Left at half-mast, the light showed me his reclining form on our C-shaped sofa set. He was facing me, his meaty build so *even*, so close to perfect proportion without even trying, covered below the waist by a thin sheet and perhaps an unseen pair of briefs. My eagle eyes told me to doubt that latter possibility very much. He wriggled his big, thuddy feet during my understandable hesitation; they peeked out at me and were the part of his body closest to me.

I had been madly in lust with Andrew since I'd first laid eyes on him one year previously. He'd shown up at my door in response to my ad in a gay rag for a platonic roommate. I could have afforded a reasonably priced penthouse with the money I made, but there's no need to flash illicit money around, so a coupla roommates seemed a prudent decision. More important, it was a year after I'd obsessed over Nervous on the Jeffery #6 and I still hadn't had sex—*real* sex with someone I *felt like* fucking. I'd decided that the best way for a busy guy to screen potential partners would be to place an ad for a "platonic" roommate. I think "platonic" is the most ironic word in the English language, even if it *is* Greek.

When I first laid eyes on Andrew, I almost lost consciousness from the sheer attraction. It wasn't all physical "What a hot stud!" desire, because there are always more physically attractive men in any number of magazines or just around any corner. I don't think there exists a man who is the most attractive of them all. If I ever find him, perhaps I will rush toward him and we will cancel each other out. I'll let you know. It wasn't that Andrew was the most classically perfect man in the world. But *I* wanted him. Lust works in mysterious ways. How can one explain a predilection for hairy men? Or black men? Or even pushy, abusive, obnoxious men? One cannot. And one should not even try. Attraction is chance.

By chance, however, Andrew was hot as the seventh plane of hell.

Unfortunately, lust is a two-way street, and Andrew hadn't even learned to drive until recently. He had worked his way up to his temporary license, and I was in the process of getting him a little road experience. With luck, I hoped to have him on the highway within the month.

What's worse, after a year of fantasizing about sleeping with Andrew and making him my boyfriend, I found myself in the unenviable position of being hopelessly, helplessly in *love* with him. Kill me now.

Here was my still platonic roommate, looking lifeless with thought. *No smile. What's wrong?*

"Well?" he prompted. I wondered if Mr. Kenna, my junior high anatomy teacher, knew the name of the muscle that flexed near Andrew's collarbone when he was testy. And shirtless.

Andrew's face was large (everything about him was "big," even intangibles like his personality and sense of humor), and imperfect, weathered here and there, a Tom Berenger-in-*Platoon*ish scar on his upper lip, uneven cheekbones, a hole in his chin. His body was a V that sometimes did a U-turn, with a small belly and love handles clinging to a solid frame. Beef. Cake.

In short, Andrew was sexy beyond words. If you can't make this connection, just stop reading now. I don't like your kind. What am I doing, telling a story or trying to explain my psyche?

I slouched, mock-exhausted, against the door (or was I trying to sink through it and escape?). "I was on a date, Andrew. And I'm dead."

He tilted his head. *Oh, Fido! Don't ask—*

"A date, or a 'date'?"

"You got an awfully smart-assed mouth for a Minnesota farm boy." I gathered myself and strolled over to him, my eyes already half-closed with bravado. The spunk I'd needed to manhandle Joe was making a belated appearance. I was suddenly pretty, witty, and gay, and capable of trying to figure out why Andrew was encased in gloom for the first time in his life.

I grasped his crossed feet—*cold!*—and tossed them off the footrest, making room for me. He spread his legs, comfortably resting one foot on either side of me on the rug. It was all too erotic, but I was used to sublimating it—I just *breathed*.

I stared into his darkened eyes. "Of course it wasn't a date. It's always a 'date' on Fridays—you know that. Why do you enjoy making me say it? Shall I stop calling them 'dates' at all and just say I was 'at work'? 'On call'?"

His lips wrinkled a little, a halfhearted smirk. There was no doubt about it—he was not his usual chipper self. Something major had occurred.

"Why not just say you were hooking?" I must've looked a little surprised, and actually I was a lot surprised. I couldn't believe he could say "hooking" so offhandedly. I'm resilient to negative prostitution words, metaphors, and references in daily conversation ("selling out," "cheap," "what a slut!"), but I didn't like hearing it so pointedly from Mr. Reduced-Rent in my own home. The repulsive irony—that I was passing up Joe, who embraced my activities as a part of my charm, and was incurably hot for puritanical Andrew—did not escape me.

"What's your point?" When cornered, I am ice.

He looked down, away. "Nothing. No point. Sorry." A string of sharp little words. He was not trying to hurt me; he was upset.

I leaned toward him, expecting to smell the musky scent of his that lingers throughout our apartment and haunts me during the day. But instead, there was beer and the salty odor of personal anguish. Death? Had someone died? I touched his shoulder with my hand, gripped it, and felt the nudity of my voice, stripped of humor and pretense.

"What is wrong, Andrew? Tell me."

He shook his head lazily, forcing a smirk on his lips. His eyes shone in the dimness.

"Stupid," he managed, "I'm just being stupid." He was breathing deeply to gain control, suddenly trying to be all guy-ish about it, shake it off, shake it off. When he raised his head again and looked into my eyes, he looked defiant—not of me, but of betraying any more emotion. "It's so *nothing*. Really. Just my, uh, last girlfriend from . . . well, my last one . . ."

I bristled a little inside, formulating a mental image of Jill, the selfish prom queen Andrew had lovingly described to me once, a girl who had dumped him after a yearlong relationship and months-long engagement when he'd refused to marry her. He'd told her he wanted to wait. Thank God he *had* waited (otherwise, he'd be out fucking guys on the sly a year after the "I do's"), and thank God he hadn't gone off the deep end when the girl's family and friends—who had been as much to Andrew, too—never spoke to him again. A woman scorned, except she didn't deserve to be called a woman. But I mustn't let my horny protectiveness blind me. In all fairness, her engagement *was* a year gone from her life . . . *Dead?* Was she *dead?*

I was mercilessly indifferent that the bitch'd died. But I acted sad out of concern for the living. My voice was no longer nude, but decked out in haute couture.

"Is she . . . dead?" I whispered, hoping against hope.

His reaction was an unsettling howl of laughter so strong, his head snapped back painfully against the wooden frame of the sofa. I broke into a cold sweat at the shocking transition from apathy to levity. His whole body tightened and convulsed with nervous glee and I shrank away defensively, a little annoyed and feeling ridiculed.

"What?" I demanded. "WHAT?"

He slowly calmed down and wiped tears from his eyes, blinking at me through a mile-wide crooked grin. "I'm sorry. Honest to God, I'm not laughing at you—it's just that when you said 'dead,' it was so fucking hilarious. She sent me an *invitation;* she's getting *married.*" He gestured to a white card on the end table and snorted a little again.

I was having none of this.

I slapped his belly smartly with my palm and started to get up indignantly. He jerked and grunted at the smack and laughed harder as he locked me in with his powerful arms. I kicked and squirmed, trying to escape him, and damn near made it away, too.

"Damn—you're a wriggly little sonofabitch!" he laughed.

Fooled, laughed at, captured, I began to giggle. "I never give it up without a fight!" He easily tossed me to the floor and pounced on me, a huge thigh at either side of me, salami-solid arms pinning my hands to the carpet. I'd forgotten about his nakedness until now, and quickly looked away from what romance writers would carefully describe as his "manhood."

Actually, "manhood" is a pretty canny term. I still call it a dick or a cock or a prick, but "manhood" comes much closer to conveying the complex array of emotions that find their gathering point in the penis, and that compel such foolhardy souls as I to worship that member in a way that embarrasses us in our more rational, guarded moments.

In a year of cohabitation and friendship so communal it bordered on marriage, I'd never seen Andrew's manhood.

Uncut! Uncut! Uncut!

"Get that fuzzy cheese factory off me!" Still playing, but playing for keeps.

His eyes lit up. *"Cheese factory?"*

"Yeah—get that hooded thing fixed—can't trust anything you can't see."

He was shocked, as always, by my vulgarity. "I—didn't know that circumcision made for a more trustworthy penis."

"Trust me," I teased, "it does."

He got a goofy look in his eyes. "Well, let's have a look . . ." and pretended to start undoing my pants. When my freed hands made no move to stop him, his expression faded to pink and he uncomfortably stopped everything by slugging my shoulder.

"OW!"

Mussing my hair, he leapt off me, nonchalantly drawing the sheet around his waist and tying it securely. He plodded around the apartment gathering his clothes from where he'd discarded them earlier. "Stupid, stupid, stupid," he kept chanting, and I sensed that the subject had changed back to his girlfriend. It had never really changed in the first place.

That was the first time I had hinted to Andrew that I wanted him badly. Andrew's response was clearly vague. He knew I'd've given it up to him, and he had shied away, that was for certain. But why? Bad timing? Disinterest in me? Or just his ongoing confusion?

Optimistically, maybe he didn't want to make me one in a list of experiments on the way to understanding his sexuality. Maybe he was saving me for later, in hopes of making me his "lover" and not just his "sex partner."

Maybe he was just upset that his girlfriend was getting married, just like all his old (straight) friends, leaving him behind, and one step closer to lifelong homosexuality.

Maybe, to him, someone *had* died.

Whatever, I could not guess his immediate agenda, but I did

suspect that Joe had not been the only one waiting up for me that night.

Suddenly, though, I felt like Joe, all exposed and desperate and worked-up and rejected.

I AM SENTI-MENTAL

Feeling inches away from bagging Andrew only to be disappointed, hurled miles away from him, made me reconsider Joe. Reconsidering Joe led straight back to one thing, one overriding reason why I felt I could never have sex with him.

Sexually speaking, there exists a great dichotomy in this world, one that surfaces continually despite all the murk involved in sex roles and mutualism: There are two types of sexual beings, tops and bottoms. Those who give, and those who receive. The fuckers, and the fucked. And if taking money for sex since age fifteen has taught me anything, it's how to tell who's who. Joe was indisputably a bottom, and that didn't do me any good.

If someone is reading this and saying, "BULL-SHIT! I like to give and get, just ask all the guys at the gym!"—*forget it.* Drop it—who are you trying to kid? Me? I'm not even *there,* I'm words on a page. You're alone with yourself, so why not admit it; you can *do* top and bottom, you can do both and get off, but when it comes right down to it, you know where you wanna be on judgment day.

Anyone in the world can switch-hit. I've fucked my brains out (literally, I sometimes fear). I've fucked the shit out of more men than I can shake my stick at. I was even able to come doing that—for a few extra bucks—but so what? I can come if the wind blows on me the right way. Coming isn't the decisive factor in what you find truly pleasurable.

So I fucked, but not by choice. I fucked for pay, but given the choice, I wanted to *get fucked*. I was and am Mr. Bottom Numero Uno, though at the time I had preserved myself for too many years to remember accurately.

Let me explain.

I loved the idea of getting screwed, or more correctly, I loved the distant, hazy memory of getting screwed, and yet had only consented to it once in my long, full life. Are you surprised? You were expecting the Lincoln Tunnel? "He's a whore—he must've been *butt*-fucked from here to there and back again." (I bet you do too say *"butt*-fuck.") Well, you're a little presumptuous for such a progressive thinker.

First, I was not promiscuous, relatively speaking, since about half the fags on the planet do it thirty-nine times a week more than I did and still find time to jerk off twice a day.

Second, and this is key, on the job I didn't take *shit* in my ass. No fingers, no tongues (*Really!* Let's be as unsafe as possible. Just go ahead and drink my blood, while you're at it. I don't care if porn stars rim. Porn stars don't have as much to live for as I do. Just ask Joey Stefano), no inanimate objects (I am not "The Blob"), and absolutely, positively, no no no penises. At all. No close calls allowed, either. Just keep it away. Hold it yourself, thank you.

Why?

I've alluded to AIDS, but AIDS would be a correct, well-informed, acceptable LIE. A cop-out. It was really only a convenient excuse for me, a good one at that.

Truth be told, I kept my hole preserved in memoriam. It was sentimental. If I'd let someone inhabit me via that sacrosanct portal, that would constitute putting him on an equal level with Andy. And have made me remember. And that just wouldn't do.

OK. All right. I can't keep going on like this—I admit it. It all goes back to Andy, everything, all of it. The whole goddamned story begins here, not on page one. Oh, *God,* I dread dredging him up. But it's all too fucking obvious. My heart's on my sleeve, and it's time to do the laundry. Here comes the answer to the question: What was your first time like?

I was thirteen.

Sweet thirteen, never been kissed. Never given a blow job, either, or taken it where it counts. I was absolutely virginal at thirteen, just emerged from a period of obesity, gawky looks, and over-all unattractiveness. What happened to me that year? God knows, or would if one existed. I simply awoke one day and gazed into the mirror and smiled—I had become firm(er), shapely, my eyes stood out and my nose sang with subtlety, my mouth was large and fun-looking, dripping perfect teeth, and I had an ass to make grown men weep. Actually, I was only a halfway beauty, but the beauty of youth was on my side. Maybe my actual transformation took longer, but it seemed to hit me all at once like this, and I'm sure I'll pay for it at some point if I haven't already.

At that time, I was old enough to "know." I certainly knew I liked other boys in my class, but I liked older men even better. And more than life itself, I loved my cousin Andy (I know, I know—"Andy"/"Andrew"—it gets worse). Before I launch into another half-lucid description of the male form, a disclaimer: I loved Andy for Andy, loved him from when he was a sturdy but unremarkably built thirteen-year-old, before he'd yawned and stretched into a voluptuous sixteen-year-old Adonis, fueled by sports and thoughtless weight lifting. Then there was his face. Like Andrew's, it was idiosyncratic, but much more commercial overall. He had dark, wavy hair (I know, but he did), crystal-blue eyes, and smiling lips. He was rock-solid, a big, masculine hunk who would nevertheless sob at overwrought TV movies of the week and heart-tugging episodes of "The Golden Girls." He even cried when his little cousin's kitten died—I'll never forgive my sisters for letting Miss Alicia Fuzz out of the house in the first place.

I was most proud that Andy was the only guy on the JV foot-ball team who'd refused to help terrorize the only Jew in school.

Andy was forever sweet, the only beauty I've ever known without even a touch of cruelty.

I saw him every single weekend at our aunt's house from practically before I was born. Aunt Dell's was where every relative clustered after church (I'm afraid) to eat a week's worth of Polish food. Andy would be the center of attention, a luscious little godling running around amid ogres, and the ogres recognized his natural "talent." They doted on him, delighted at his tales of knocking down straight B-minuses in school and still making first string.

The only string I gave a damn about was the one holding his sweats up.

I always sat at the big dinner table with Andy directly across from me, watching him choke down halved potatoes and pieces of meat as large as small dinosaurs. He would have a look of oblivious good-naturedness on his face as he chewed and laughed and told stories.

And *every* three minutes to the goddamned second, *every* three minutes, he would lift his eyes and stare at me with a secretive smile. Our camaraderie was unchallenged, and his glances were all-important to me, delicious reminders that we were together through all the family clutter and chatter and all their singling out of him. I would eat my asparagus deliberately, considering how good it would be to taste even one salty inner thigh, to make him moan and rage and lose it—deliver unto him the ecstasy he, by the right of his goodness and beauty, deserved. My mouth—deliverer of justice! But more than my mouth, what was this happy-go-lucky feeling in my ass?

On one of these days—pick any one, I don't think it matters which—the unthinkable happened. It was weird because I remember knowing it was going to happen that day as soon as I saw him at Aunt Dell's.

My parents had been bickering over the frequency of our family visits to Aunt Dell's, "Centerfold" by the J. Geils Band was number one on Casey Kasem, my sisters—well, *that's* another story. But like JFK day for the oldies, the details of this day are with me even now, even if the date has escaped me.

Andy was in bathing trunks—bright pink because pink was so "in" that year for regular guys, regular guys suddenly dressed well and listened to New Wave. He wore an ancient T-top, large arms sporting a peeling tan, great big lusty grin.

I have this theory that queers have a sixth sense in detecting other queers, with or without their consent. The sense works rather more like a set of antennae, constantly wiggling in every direction, receiving invisible data from all points and broadcasting the findings down into our heads. Since I first dreamed up this concept when sex was *everything* to me, and since sex is *still* everything to me, I've dubbed these "sex antennae."

Andy was radiating energy, and my still fledgling sex antennae twitched expectantly. Something was up.

Small talk—macho banter, really—between my dad and Andy and then we were all sucked into the teeming familial mass of over-made-up aunts and slothlike uncles prostrate on sofas watching TV. Talk talk talk and thousands of small children running around while their still youngish parents eyed each other's spouses and spouses' siblings, sizing each other up sexually just for fun. Baby jam-bo-REE. More babies than humanly digestible. The smell of cabbage wafted from a kitchen sagging with immobile grandmas and their papier-mâché mothers, who sat draped in forty-year-old cocktail dresses. Ah, family!

After an hour, when everyone was at their busiest, greeting, laughing, slapping backs, and positioning themselves in the area where the food line was about to form, Andy and I ended up downstairs in the TV room. It was a world apart, that TV room, because it was impossible for small children and the elderly to get to it. That flight of stairs down was steeper than a rope ladder. The room itself was "refinished," another big thing to do that year, but smelled dank from being a converted basement. There was stubbly carpeting, and lots of enormous, harmlessly stained pillows we'd lie around on, talking about "Charlie's Angels," "CHiPs," "Three's Company," Atari, school, junk. We were so secluded that the upstairs noise was reduced to a surreal murmur, and at some point during our dialogue, the noise was smothered completely.

"I have a girlfriend now," Andy said.

Since the last thing he'd said was in reference to Pac Man, I was fazed by this proclamation. And I could've bawled my eyes out if I weren't being watched.

"What?" Still shockable at this point in my life, I picked up my nonplussedness later, the minute I set foot in a gay bar.

"I said I have a girlfriend now," Andy repeated. He was looking at me, smiling with affected snobbery. He arched his eyebrows (I loved those things) and sucked air through his teeth. "Yep, yep, yep." Richie Cunningham mannerisms, but Richard Gere package.

"Who?" Quick as ever.

He turned toward me, propping his head up on his palm, sinking halfway into the pillow next to mine. His biceps bulged obscenely, and I imagined the existence of God as a very mean-spirited queen, having a hoot at my expense. "Jennifer," he said. *What a fucking bland name—so popular!* "Jenny, actually." *Worse!*

"What's she look like?" I was all ears, eyes, nose, and throat, very raw and exposed-feeling. I was not going to cry, unless he said . . .

"A whole lot better than you," he laughed, reaching over and mussing my hair. A fake laugh, at least, no true hilarity. My eyes were so hot and full and my stomach so sick, I didn't think I'd remain conscious. I had dreaded this moment since I was ten, maybe even before, but ten was when I had first perceived females as a threat to our little fraternity, and now, after three short years, we were finally, inevitably, being torn asunder by a *girl*. How could my sex antennae have been so wrong? Far from succumbing, he was dropping me like deadweight. Up, up, and away. *So long, squirt.*

"No, I'm just kidding." He smiled, closing his eyes lazily. "I'll always like you better than her. We've been best friends forever and I'm not going to drop off the face of the earth just because I'm dating a girl."

"Sure took you long enough," I chirped before I knew what I was chirping.

Andy's eyes opened and looked crosswise at me. "And just what is that supposed to mean?"

I got a taste of what sheer pleasure it is to drop little word bombs on the unsuspecting, then clam up to torture them even more.

"Nothin'." I rolled away and off of the big pillow, a smile on my lips as I lay motionless on the cool carpet. I've got you now, Mr. Footballs.

Andy repeated his question. Then, after my continued silence, "Well? What do you mean, 'took you long enough'?"

"You're sixteen years old, Andy."

"So?"

Silence. *Silence.*

"SO? So what? Are you saying I'm too old to have a girlfriend?"

"No," I said calmly, "you're never too old for *that*. What I'm saying is that most guys start dating when they're *my* age, Andy. Most guys are practically married by the time they're *your* age . . ."

He howled. "Listen to you! Trying to embarrass me for being a late bloomer."

"No," I replied, "you aren't a late bloomer, Andy. You bloomed on time. What I'm saying is it sure took a long, long, long, long-*ass* time for you to notice girls." When that had sunk in, "And I was just wondering why the sudden interest. Pressure getting to you? Afraid the family will be wondering why Mr. Perfect doesn't have a Miss?"

Andy grabbed me by the arm and jerked me over to face him, his face clouded with confusion and anger. "What the fuck are you saying? Why are you being such an asshole about this? I'm only telling you I have a girlfriend—OK, 'finally' have a girlfriend—because you're the only person I trust enough to tell about it. I don't care what those assholes upstairs have to say and I'd just as soon they didn't even know I *have* a girlfriend. They know almost everything else there is to know about me already, and they still want to know more. My goddamned report card is taped on the fridge by the serving line, for crissakes!"

He faltered, laughed a little, nervously, trying to lighten up what had started out as a knock-down, drag-out tell-off. I wasn't placated and refused to laugh along with him. He was still holding my arm firmly, and I didn't like the idea of him tossing me around so easily. *What am I saying?*

"I'm sorry," I said woodenly, "I'm just teasing you—"

"Well, don't," he interrupted. "You're always teasing me, saying little things to bug me, and I don't like it."

Unaware he'd ever caught any of my little gibes, I asked him why they bothered him.

"It makes me feel slow. You make me feel stupid sometimes." He loosened his grip on me. "I know you don't mean to, but you do. You're a lot smarter than me and you know it, and you rub it in without even trying."

Andy was never one for speeches, but he was certainly making up for lost time that afternoon. The guys on the football team would retch. As for me, I was inflamed.

"I . . . never knew I did that," I replied. "I'm sorry . . ." Andy was distracted, having noticed the red mark on my arm from where he'd grabbed me.

"Fuck—I'm sorry; I didn't mean to grab you like that."

And then it happened.

Andy was sort of snorting at his clichéd apology and looking around sheepishly, and then he looked at me dead-on, blue-blue eyes. I guess I couldn't conceal my own willingness any more than he could suppress his, because he seemed to perceive in my eyes that it was okay for him to do it. He nudged forward on his elbows, leaned a hot cheek against mine, nuzzling me tentatively, then kissed my lips with his, breathing heavily against my face. I felt weightless and afraid, like I just got sucked out of an airplane at thirty thousand feet. I remember how strange and exciting it was to feel his tongue on my lips and in my mouth, caressing my teeth. We were kissing like it was going out of style, and *who knows?* maybe it was.

I remember a lot of things about that afternoon, every single thing we did in the thirty-six or -seven minutes we dared to spend making love downstairs, separated from every relative we ever had by one cheap, homemade door that led to the binge above. I remember more about his body than I've managed to figure out about my own, and I remember feeling the one thing I haven't felt since, the nasty thrill of being taken and taken again.

Well, well, well.

Anal sex is so abstract. It's not at all like any novice would ever be able to imagine it. It's not necessarily messy or bloody (please!), and more than anything, it doesn't have to hurt one bit. If there is a single part of your being that resents the intrusion, it will hurt proportionately. If you are completely physically and mentally and emotionally prepared, it's blissful proportionately. It's a delicious severance from yourself, a deliverance from that feeling of abdominal guardedness. The tightness goes away (though hopefully not completely) and you are left basking in utterly defenseless relaxation. What could be sexier? Sex isn't about intensity of physical stimulation, but about degree of abandon. The extent to which you can *let yourself go*.

And I was out of the fucking ballpark!

Listen to me; I sound ridiculous. I guess it's OK for me to be a little self-conscious about this now. After all, I wasn't self-conscious when it counted.

Suffice it to say that the experience was like a tattooing. I will always carry it on me (not with me, but *on* me), whether I like it or not. And lately, I like it more than I did for those first few years afterward. Leave it to a gay guy to charge sex with such sentimentality.

We stopped reluctantly when our three-year-old third cousin opened the upstairs door and screamed violently, probably for no reason at all since it was impossible to see us from that angle. All I can say is THANK GOD we were not in the act, because you always hear those hospital emergency room horror stories. "Doctor, I have a little problem . . . This is my friend Butchie, by the way . . . We're kind of stuck together . . ." Just like Suzanne Somers in *Hollywood Wives*.

By the time the scream came, we had, too. Twice apiece, a feat I have yet to surpass since, despite what any porno movie or bragging acquaintance has ever purported. It's just me, I guess, but alone I don't see the point after twice, and none of my clients had ever paid for a double.

MATTHEW RETTENMUND

You have noticed, I'm sure, how chatty I've gotten in the last paragraphs. I apologize and will admit I am stalling. Sue me. Flip ahead if you're that impatient. Points will be taken off for rudeness.

Afterward, we cleaned up and suddenly reverted to the sheepish stage that had immediately preceded the penetration stage.

"That was cool," Andy mumbled.

"Yeah," I agreed.

"I've wanted to," he continued.

"I know . . . Me, too." I smiled, looked around. "Obviously."

"So . . . I don't know what this means."

It was my first experience with sorting out emotions after already having sex, so I didn't recognize the early warning. When they are perplexing over what it all means before the semen dries, that usually means that they enjoyed it immensely, but aren't comfortable with that fact. I didn't know any better, so I was bending over backwards (sue me again) to please him.

"I don't either. Whatever you want it to mean. I love you."

Oh, man!

He gripped my shoulders a little distantly. "I love you, too. I love ya a lot. I want to do more. I like it . . ." *Oh, the sincerity!*

"But . . ."

That "but" dangled between us while the house settled on its foundations noisily around us. But but but. *But.*

"But?" My blood ran cold, my ass still wet and raw.

"But . . . I don't know."

"I don't give a *fuck* what you 'know.' " I pulled up my pants, fumbled with my belt. "You *said* you loved me, so what's the problem?"

How about: Statutory rape? Incest? Homosexuality? All of the above?

Don't forget I was awfully young then. At first I was sure his reticence was about admitting to being gay. I wish I were so sure about that now, but the fact is, I may have been underestimating Cousin Andy all these years. It was probably about a lot more than homosexuality. Maybe it was sexuality in general.

His eyes were dull, a muted expression on his face that you might recognize as the "I'm about to dump you for no good reason" look.

"I loved you before today and I'll keep on loving you, no more, no less, but . . ."

" *'No more'? You stick your dick* inside *me and you say you feel the same way about me as you always have?*" I screamed, shrill as a bat and looking for some hair to tangle myself in. I lost control of my body for the second time that afternoon (counting the whole sexual experience once instead of twice, since each orgasm represented merely a slight peak in my general lost-it-ness). I was in the "destroy" mode.

Andy put a hand over my mouth hard enough to make me bite my tongue, wrapped the other around my waist, and pulled me into him, this time coldly, asexually, out of self-preservation.

"Shut up! Jesus Christ! Everyone's going to come running down here!"

Did he really care? Or was he more afraid of what *I'd* say to him?

I struggled against him to no avail and finally lost my battle with tears. I'd been set to cry because he had some dork girlfriend, and now I was crying because my entire life had just taken a decidedly ugly turn, had been ripped away from me, chewed up, spit out. He started trying to console me more affectionately, stroking my hair, but I was repulsed, hate giving me that extra ounce of power that allowed me to topple the mighty athlete and land on him hard enough to leave him breathless.

The rest, as they say, is history. I was upstairs, outside, and out of sight before anyone knew what had happened. I started sprinting, then walking, the sixteen miles to home, unrealistically but with admirable determination. I made it, too, making sure to walk far enough away from the road to avoid the cars that eventually came in search of me.

I didn't cry again until two presidents later.

Andy didn't come looking for me. I later found out he'd run after me and then had retired to his room for the evening. He pretty much retired from life, too. Oh, he didn't commit suicide or anything. Fags don't *have* to do that anymore. He just stopped *living*. He plunged into sports more than ever, got a scholarship, moved away. They say he's heading for the pros, too, whatever that means.

He married Jennifer last June, and needless to say, that was one union I did not attend. Oh, if I could've been flower girl, I might have done it. But then, I couldn't have been flower girl. I would've been the best man there.

I've not laid eyes on Andy since that day, except more recently in photos of him I caught in an errant sports section.

After that day, everyone in the family was convinced I was crazy, running off like that for no reason, turning up home in the pitch black. My parents (especially my mom, who inwardly cheered) were very willing to accept my refusal to go to Aunt Dell's ever again. Aunt Dell's heart was broken, but hey, it's a tough life. Nothing personal.

I AM
CURIOUS

After Andy, Andrew, Joe, and myself—not necessarily in that order—I'd have to say that the most important person in my life was Gregory. Gregory was one of my clients, but he was also an invaluable teacher and friend. An impeccably well-groomed and charmingly mannered gentleman of eighty, he still cut a striking figure when reclining—he was the only client I ever fellated, and I'm a little nervous to admit that I also swallowed with him once. If you think it's hard to dissuade a horny young muscle-boy from coming unbidden in your mouth, let me tell you it's just *depressing* to deny an ancient. Russian roulette with protein.

Gregory originally came to me via Lucy, the waitress at the one tiny Italian *caffè* in Hyde Park. Moda Fromaggia was about one block away from where I'd lived all through my lost college years, and I'd spent many free evenings dining there with a book along the lines of *The Andy Warhol Diaries* or *The Matt Dillon Quiz Book* or *Understanding the Male Prostitute*.

Lucy was an old souse, a squishy ole lady who could sit you down and learn your entire life story complete with intimate secrets in five minutes. She thought she'd done that with me, but in reality all she'd learned was that I was a hustler. With that jewel of a secret in her beak, she told me two things. One: Safe sex. Two: She gets 20 percent on all referrals. I told her I'd give her 25 percent on any referral I actually used, since I wasn't really in the market for new bodies, and even when one of my dozen or so clients moved away, died, or disappeared without a trace, I was ridiculously choosy in selecting a replacement.

Just after John the black clothier and family man died suddenly of a heart attack (his wife informed me, finding my phone number in his address book and assuming I was one of *his* customers), Lucy called me with her first and only referral.

"There's this old guy," she whispered conspiratorially into the receiver, "and all the U-of-C kids say he's *queer*." To Lucy, the University of Chicago's students attended some mystical place called "Youvsee," and "queer" was the old-fashioned way of saying "gay." As queer radicals began to sprout up across the world, good old Lucy was so behind the times in her terminology that she was actually cutting edge. You know what they say about waiting long enough until things come back in fashion; who'd've thought a slur would return as a weapon?

"He lives in the dorm across from Lake Shore, the old hotel they converted to dorms in the sixties."

According to legend, all of the original residents of what had been a residence/hotel were given the choice to stay on, but most took to the hills. Why would middle-aged people want to live in a building being converted into a dorm? Whether out of fear of relocating, plain stubbornness, or perhaps a desire to be among vital young students, there were still a handful of real old folks living in a few of the corner rooms of the Lake Shore, thirty years after the first egghead freshmen had descended upon the place. One of these lifelong residents, it seemed, was this old guy Mr. Knopf.

Gregory Knopf had come into Moda for years, and Lucy had always suspected he fancied boys, watching him watching some of the dishwashers. After overhearing some frat lunks dishing on the old guy, Lucy took it upon herself to befriend Gregory, chatting him up and finding him to be a wildly entertaining, extremely frank, and desperately lonely man. In discussing her only queer comrade (me), she'd brought up my work, and Gregory had produced his card with a wink.

I couldn't resist the opportunity to meet Gregory after Lucy's gushing appraisal. She made him sound like a genuinely interesting man, and I was also morbidly intrigued by the idea of having sex with an octogenarian. Would he be stiff and short of breath? Wrinkled and liver-spotted? Would I be screwing a mummy?

I met Gregory in his decidedly large and expertly cluttered suite on the top floor of the old Lake Shore, first an opulent hotel whose grand ballroom saw Teddy Roosevelt's daughter wed, and later a ritzy lake-view residential manor for the young and bored. As of late—approximately a year before I was *born*—the Lake Shore was merely a dormitory for mostly privileged, unilaterally snobbish geniuses with no social lives and even fewer manners. Gone were the days of glamour, rudely displaced by vulgarity, youth, and short-hair, multipurpose polyester carpeting.

Nobody looked at me twice as I strolled in and all the way up to Gregory's rooms. I wasn't so far removed from college as to raise security's suspicions. To them I was merely another white prepster, a potential complaint that my water pressure wasn't satisfactory.

Gregory appeared at the door, framed by a magnificent lake view that would've commanded thousands a month were it not snug as a bug on the notorious South Side of Chicago, albeit in cozy Hyde Park.

"Hello, hello!" he greeted me exuberantly, John Gielgud with springier joints. "Please come inside."

Gregory looked sixty, not eighty, clad in a neat little cardigan that matched his pants, shoes, shirt, and ring. He was a vision of autumn in browns, grays, subtle lavender, and rust. His shock of wintery yellow-white hair was the logical complement to his September smile. Gee, "September Smile" sounds like a lost Carpenters single. All in all, Gregory was an attractive old goat from the get-go.

Gregory's apartment was packed with books and adorned with prints of birds, cats, mice—all things small and alive with tiny, thumping hearts. He seated me on a divan that might have once seated a revolutionary general and his mistress, then disappeared to fetch me an Evian and himself an iced tea.

"So." He smiled, returning with our drinks. "Tell me about your life—I want to know the course our romance will take."

I sipped and parried. "I'm not sure what Lucy told you, but we won't exactly be having a romance."

"Well, certainly we will." Gregory was quite adamant on this point. "Of course, I realize I will pay you—handsomely for such a handsome boy—" (I attempted to blush) "—for sex. This I know. But surely a lad of your experience—you've probably been doing this for a *decade* by now—" (I attempted not to kill him) "—surely you realize that it's impossible to have sex without having romance."

I laughed aloud and Gregory laughed with me, though he clearly meant what he was saying.

"We'll see, Gregory, we'll see."

I usually spent every Saturday morning at Gregory's, three hours of conversation that at first unsettled and then engaged me. His powers of observation rivaled my own, his knowledge of the lives of his surrounding student neighbors so complete, it seemed he'd been a fly on all of their walls simultaneously.

"The girl in 612 is *pregnant*," he said once, eyes wide with alarm, "and she's fool enough to believe that she can actually have the baby and return to school once it enters kindergarten." He clucked his tongue. "God didn't invent abortions for nothing, you know. A mess . . . a tragedy . . . but what else? An eighteen-year-old mother? Can you imagine? Of course you can—they're all around. I just wish people could be infertile until they're thirty when they'd make better parents anyway. Her mother is the one who convinced her not to have an abortion. I happen to know that her mother slept with one of the security men here when she visited on Parent's Day." He stopped to munch a soda cracker. "Typical Catholic—all talk, no morals."

Gregory didn't ask for sex at first. When I brought it up, he pooh-poohed me. "Patience, young lover, patience. Our time will come. But before I take you to bed, I'm going to make you want it at least half as much as I do."

Every time we met he had a stiffie as he tore a check from his ledger. I always left confused, but richer, less Lucy's 25 percent.

I AM
AN OPEN
BOOK

The morning after Andrew's melancholy could have been Armageddon and I wouldn't have known. People could've been running around tearing their eyes out and screaming as seven-headed dragons danced down Lake Shore Drive, but I was sound asleep until three o'clock P.M. I was drained from dodging Joe and from Andrew dodging me. All that fencing takes a lot out of a guy.

I opened my eyes to find Andrew perched Native-American-style in the chair next to my bed, brow scrunched up from the effort of reading a book. Stephen King, not surprisingly. Andrew's reading table looks like a Top Ten Best-Sellers list.

"What are you doing?" I grumped, layers of slime on me and in me after such a long sleep.

He looked up at me and cocked his head. "You slept three days. It's Monday."

"Ha." I rolled over. *Wanna join me?*

"I was waiting for Cinderella to open her eyes so Prince Charming could extend a formal invitation."

When I turned to him, it was my turn to have scrunched brows. "Cinderella didn't sleep—Sleeping Beauty slept. But you wouldn't know that since all you read is about animated corpses and ax murderers." He leapt onto the bed and started tickling the fuck out of me in much the same manner as our wrestling match from the previous night. I'm not ticklish, I just *hate* being tickled.

Did he never learn? He's lucky he didn't nudge the wrong leg because I had just woken up from one sex dream and into another.

I told him in my mean voice to stop and he stopped. "Well . . . aren't you going to ask me what the invite is to?"

"What?" *Snore.*

"Well, it's a formal event . . ."

I cracked an eye open. He was enjoying this immensely, his previously absent smile now making up for its disappearance in spades. The ape was also stretching out my red silk pajama bottoms, a gift from a judge with good taste. I grinned back devilishly.

"Not that I *mind* you being in my pants," I said through clenched teeth, "but would you please tell me why you're wearing those in my room reading a book while waiting for me to wake up? Spit it out."

He leaned down until he was whispering in my ear, the physical closeness flooding my senses with false expectations. I am convinced they do that on purpose sometimes.

"The pajamas I found in the hamper—fair game." Cute how Andrew treated my dirty clothes hamper as a Goodwill bin. "The book I borrowed from your apprentice, Joe. The reason I'm waiting for you is that I'm excited and a little nervous about the question I have to ask you."

The crack about Joe suggested he knew the score there. Perhaps Andrew was more alert than I usually gave him credit for. The truth is, Andrew wasn't stupid; I just wanted him to be so he couldn't fuck my life up so easily.

"Yes, I'll marry you."

He crossed his arms disapprovingly. "Actually, that's not a bad guess. A wedding is involved, but not ours. I, uh, want you to come with me to my, uh, girlfriend's wedding."

I pulled the covers over my head in time to have them pulled off again. "No way!"

"Why?" I could tell I would be going to this wedding, like it or not. "I'm asking you as a friend to come with me because this will be very hard for me. I don't like the idea that Jill's getting married, even though I don't care about her that way anymore. But I have a feeling that if I go, I'll be leaping a tall hurdle."

"Where do I come in?"

"You, I will need for support. A coach. You're the one who took me to the bars, you're the one who introduced me to the first man I ever did anything with . . ."

It was true, believe it or not. I had taken him to a party that an alderman friend of mine was throwing, a little gay shindig, and watched helplessly as an Andrew-clone swept Andrew off his feet and into an upstairs bedroom. Had there been a pistol in the house, I would've killed them both, then everyone else just out of spite. He didn't even end up liking the experience very much. The guy had been weird in bed, so Andrew said, though I couldn't get him to say what he meant by "weird." As green as Andrew was, oral sex might have seemed exotic.

I never got the whole story, but what remained in my mind was when Andrew hugged me later, at home, and told me, "Even though I just can't talk about all of this right now, just having you here is so important to me. Thanks, guy—you're the greatest."

There had even been other men in Andrew's life, usually short, ill-conceived, and disappointing affairs. The only affair of substance had lasted four months and saw me gain twenty pounds and take up smoking. I quit smoking when Andrew quit his boyfriend, and I lost twenty-*two* pounds, thank you very much.

I myself never made overt passes at Andrew not because I was the "greatest," but because I knew he would have turned me down. I would never allow anyone to humiliate me so. Submission is one thing, but *hey*. I could sense he was always considering the possibility of sex with me, but that something was holding him back. His occasionally negative opinion of my career seemed a likely candidate. So a year's cohabitation had gone by with no passes . . . just plays. It was a great comfort to me when Andrew confessed that he had never done more than mutual JO with his boyfriend, that he wasn't emotionally ready to do more yet. Jerking off just does not count as sex, so I could still be Andrew's first.

Everyone has a different definition of what counts as sex. At college, there were three Korean girls—roommates—who swore to me that any activity on the planet that didn't involve the breakage of their hymens left them virgins. This made them three exceptionally fun dates whose sexual vitae included ass-fucking, lesbianism, and oral sex for *miles*. In light of how ridiculous I found them, I can't justify not considering hand jobs to be "real" sex. It was just convenient for me at the time to think of Andrew as a virgin. Cut me that much slack.

Back to the wedding. "For the second time in two days, *What is your point, Andrew?*" He shrugged. "And what makes you think I'd be into this idea? What if someone *says* something? What if you don't realize how *obvious* we're gonna look showing up at a wedding arm in arm?"

Andrew brushed it off excitedly. "So what? Let 'em figure it out. In fact—" he narrowed his eyes shrewdly, sweetening the deal "—I hereby give you permission—"

"*Permission?* He gives me *permission* now!" I was just teasing.

"If you'll let me finish; I hereby give you permission to be my openly gay date. I'm asking you on a date here."

The plot quickened. "We can flame through Hadley, Minnesota?"

Rapid-fire. "Yep. Blowtorch."

"I can say whatever I want?"

"Yep. Say away."

"Do whatever I want?"

"Please do."

"And talk about inappropriately queer subjects at breathtakingly inopportune moments?"

Andrew threw his hands up. "Yes! Yes! Yes! It can be a regular demonstration if you want, or more subtle and manipulative."

We shared a deep, malevolent chuckle. The idea of dropping hints about a gay relationship to the Hadleyites was even more wickedly appealing than stomping through their town square in drag. Everyone would be abuzz: "Are they or aren't they?" The only downside, of course, was that we *weren't*. Still, it could be fun, sort of like doing it in my own hometown, except with the safety that I didn't know a soul in Hadley. And I had to believe this was some sort of easing-into for Andrew, a dress rehearsal for a relationship. Nothing wrong with practice, so long as it leads to perfection.

He made cow eyes for me, and I reluctantly agreed to rent a car and drive to the southern tip of Minnesota in order to attend the wedding of a woman whose imaginary demise I had so recently cheered.

It was up to me to rent the wheels since I was the rich one in this situation. I was so used to free wining and dining on the job that I actually enjoyed the role reversal. Maybe that's why I let him pay reduced rent, too. Hmmm. A latent sugar daddy.

Andrew was giddy with nerves at the prospect of going to the wedding, and Andrew giddy was a sight to see. He walked around on his tiptoes smiling goofily, breaking into a little jig while performing tasks like opening a can of peaches and making himself some coffee. He's so full of spark, so open-hearted in a way I can't imagine being (and often sneer at in others). That's one thing that made me *loooove* him. Ugh. While he jigged, I wished he'd come over and dance *on* me, face-to-face on the bed, if only to rub some of that energy off on me.

But more, I think I was nuts for Andrew because he was so *normal*. He read number one best-sellers, had a steady job, wore dirty clothes out of hampers, shopped at the Gap, had ex-girlfriends. Had *friends*. He was the kind of guy who spent an hour and a half on the phone with his mom every Friday, just catching up. He was the son my parents never had, and he was more like Andy than I cared to admit. I coveted that normalcy, that normalcy and that *happy-to-be-aliveness*. And that bossiness. And his chest, don't forget the chest.

And Andrew *is* smart, but his attention span is very sit-comish. Twenty-two minutes and commercials, and he's on to the next part of his life. His job was perfectly suited to him—he man-aged the Blockbuster Video store where he worked. Watch until you're bored, pause. If I had a dime for every free movie I saw around that time, I could've just bribed Andrew to ball me.

Andrew had actually met Jill at a mom-and-pop video store

in Hadley. Now she was marrying a cousin of hers, a thug whom Andrew had always feared during his relationship with the girl. The bridegroom, Abe to you, had always shown up at Jill's parties and seemed more than passingly interested in her. Jill played it off as Andrew's overactive imagination, but anyone who knows Andrew knows he *has* no imagination, so there goes that theory. Andrew had eventually let it go because Abe had joined the army and gone off to greater glory liberating Panama. They even thought he'd been killed for about a month, until it turned out he'd gone AWOL instead. He actually got a discharge after his psychiatric examination. Rumor had it he wore his yellow "Support our troops" ribbon until it faded into a white "Senior citizen rights" ribbon.

Jill and Abe were bound to have beautiful kids. After all, what incest didn't take care of, hereditary insanity would handle.

I hopped in the shower, amusing myself with the thought that I was going to be Andrew's *date* at a hick wedding. Andrew had given me the green light! I could tell everyone that Andrew and I were gay and could even lead them to believe we were lovers if I wanted to. It was the next step in his record-breaking coming-out process. That entailed possible danger, considering the groom's reputation and the fact that the crowd for a wedding whose reception would take place in a Moose hall would probably not be very into the gay sex scene. But when you live to be twenty-five and you haven't had good sex in a while, you positively *itch* for a little fun. I was game.

When I stepped out of the shower and into jeans and a rugby shirt, I heard Andrew talking outside in the living room. Either his mother had called or the landlord was noticing I had replaced the rotting door to our apartment with a glaring white one—call me fussy.

Imagine my surprise when I found Joe in the living room talking with my Andrew. Sure, he lived there, but he rarely came over to the common room, preferring to hibernate in his own space or perhaps divining my subtle annoyance at having him underfoot at times.

"Why, Joe." *Why, Joe?* "What brings you over here? Wanna borrow something?" *Andrew?*

I did not like seeing the two of them in the same frame, Andrew in shameless silk pajama bottoms and Joe in a shameless jogging outfit—black spandex shorts, a white shortie T-shirt, red tennis shoes with no socks. Between them, they had on less clothes than I had *underneath* mine.

"No, nothing really," he chirped. "I was just asking Andrew if he would get me a movie tonight."

All About Joe?

"Which one?"

Andrew beamed. "This little kid wants me to get him porno."

"I'm of age." Joe went along with the joke. Blockbuster doesn't even carry porno. Just sex comedies.

"How old *are* you, Joe?" Suddenly Andrew was Joe's biographer.

"Seventeen and a half."

It was hard to believe sometimes that Joe didn't intentionally try to be cute. Bimboism is *not* gender-specific. At that moment, all he needed was a cap with a propeller. All I needed was a blunt instrument.

Joe flirted with *everyone*, which doesn't mean I was used to him flirting with Andrew. I can be very possessive. Either that, or I'm just a bitch.

"Hey, Andrew tells me you're going to a wedding next week."

I sat on the enormous throne I'd rescued from a defunct fun house and started glancing through the comics, but I couldn't find anything that didn't look normal compared to the scene taking place around me. L'il Abner over there was watching my reaction to Joe with amusement.

"Yes, that's right. I'm his date. Should be fun." Rat-a-tat-tat.

I was not cutting Joe any slack and wasn't feeling especially cruel about it. I did not like him muscling in here. I had an enormous amount of affection for the tyke, but he was an emotional dilemma on two legs. His crush on me made him a walking, talking mirror image of myself in my struggles with Andrew. And he was sexually attractive jailbait for good measure.

Joe's face registered his perception of the situation. He knew he wasn't wanted.

"Well, let me know how it turns out." He shrugged and grinned and bade us farewell, half jogging out the door. Andrew's gaze seemed to linger on him a little longer than necessary, a thoughtful flicker in his eyes. But then it's hard not to scope an exhibitionist, if only for the carnival sideshow element of it.

I was pretty boxed-up by all this, paranoically worried that Andrew would suddenly be charmed by Joe, which wasn't difficult to do. The primary colors of the comics splashed around in front of me as I tried to focus on a single panel. This struggle lasted about *two seconds*.

"How long have you known that Joe wants me?" I asked angrily, tossing the paper aside.

Andrew had closed the door, leaning against it when he was through, effectively sealing it and keeping the outside irrevocably out. He looked massive against the tall, white door. Maybe I had subconsciously replaced the old door just to provide a better frame for Andrew when he indulged in this, one of his most consistent poses. He cocked his head and smiled with amazing restraint, not the usual shower of pearls. Uh-oh . . .

"As long as I've known that *you* want *me*."

I AM
A
ROMANTIC

Later that evening, I was reclining on Gregory's quaintest love seat, enjoying a moment of peace after twenty minutes of conversation. My eye was drawn to a photograph, a stunning sepia portrait in a brass frame. The two-dimensional face could've served as an archetype of male beauty, a dark-skinned man with a broad jaw and strong features: deep-set eyes, wavy, brilliantined hair, full lips with no hint of mirth but with the unquestionable promise of prowess and a possible reserve of tenderness, eyebrows till tomorrow.

"Who's that?" I asked lazily while Gregory watched me. "Was that your husband?"

He didn't answer right away, and when I turned I caught the tail end of a puzzled expression. For the second time in two days I had innocently asked a loaded question about an enigmatic photograph.

"Well, yes. I guess he was my husband," Gregory sighed. He paused, then continued in a mad dash of words. "He was my lover for many, many years and I loved him deeply. We lived here together for a quarter of a century. We had a love affair for about thirty years prior to his coming to live here. Yes, I could call him 'husband' . . . He certainly wasn't my *boyfriend*."

"Wow." I was impressed. A (quick math, fingertips tapping mechanically) fifty-five-year relationship between two men. Most gay guys feel married after two weeks. I myself had never had a relationship at all yet. Not *one*. But my dowry was damned impressive.

"Renaldo," he trilled, reading my mind. "A man who kept me guessing over his true feelings until the day he moved in. Once he divorced and actually lived with me, I knew once and for all he loved me."

"A divorcé?"

"Yes, yes!" he laughed, eyes disappearing in glee. Then, "You see, Renaldo and I were actually lovers here in the Lake Shore when we were kids, but he went through many . . . mood swings . . . and ended up marrying a woman he loved as a sister, going through the motions of having children and finally forsaking them . . . for me."

Too much! Suddenly Andrew seemed trivial. Renaldo sounded like Andrew squared. I knew I'd be at wits' end if Andrew got married. I looked on Gregory with renewed respect and—after a second glance at the photo of Renaldo—envy. Gregory was a hot senior citizen, but to bag Renaldo, he must have been a teen Valentino once upon a time.

Gregory beamed. "I haven't talked about Renaldo for years— he died in August of 'eighty-two, and none of our mutual friends are still alive except his brother. He's in no physical condition to reminisce, no condition at *all*." Visions of speechless, agonizing, paralytic old age.

Gregory left and returned with some piping hot lamb stew for us. The food was mysteriously familiar, almost like what the dining halls used to feed me, except tasty. As we ate, I listened to Gregory tell me how he met Renaldo, lost in a love story more complicated than my own. Forgive Gregory his treacly narrative. I did, at the time.

Gregory was born and raised until he was fifteen in England, hence the still tonicky hints of an accent. His parents had been aristocrats, young and boring chinless snobs who refused to work simply because their impending inheritances were tidy enough to allow it. They moved to America to be with their own parents, who co-owned a company that had moved to the place where it was most profitable—Chicago.

The Knopfs moved into the Lake Shore in the late twenties to a spacious suite that they would spend the next thirty years stocking with unimaginative antiques and stuffy works of art.

Gregory was frightened at the endless differences between England and America, the animalistic place he'd been told had once belonged to England until its monstrous citizens stole it back by force.

Little Gregory was fascinated by black children, whom he was able to observe up close for the first time in his life. These black children were from middle-class families living in Hyde Park and were terribly American, very brassy and full of a vigor that Gregory found absent from his memories of chummy old England. There was no question that Gregory was *not* to mix with the black children—his experiences with them were confined to moments in the backs of candy stores or unchaperoned minutes in the small park in front of the Lake Shore. Even as an adolescent, he had sought out things that were, in some way, *different.*

Forbidden, too, were any sort of egalitarian exchanges with the Latino families who worked at the Lake Shore as doormen, cooks, and janitors. From the very first, Gregory was in love with what he called "their kind banter, exquisite looks, and honest work ethic." Even more than the blacks, whom his father hated so much he never stopped talking of them, Gregory loved the Latinos, whom his father considered unremarkable.

Renaldo's father was Cuban, his mother Italian. He was a boy one year younger than Gregory, but already obviously more physically mature at fourteen. Gregory had watched Renaldo from the time he'd moved into the Lake Shore, never guessing the reason behind his intense preoccupation with the other boy.

"I remember the first day I knew I wanted Renaldo sexually," Gregory told me, his thin smile breaking into an unrestrained grin. "I can't forget it because it was also the first day he fucked me." When I tittered at his delightful disregard for romanticism, Gregory added, "Make no mistake: the only worthwhile sex is when both parties are doing it to please themselves first, each other second. But you know that. You're a whore—you know that men have the best sex of their lives with you, but that you don't enjoy it at all. That's because you're doing it all for them, and none of it for you."

My silence shocked me, and Gregory steamrolled ahead with his story.

"I'll never forget the day—it was terrifically stormy outside, the waves on the lake were louder than the thunder itself, washing into the park so that we were on alert in case we had to evacuate. I was only fifteen, just beginning to feel confident enough to suspect I was a whole separate person from my parents. I was annoyed that the weather had cut short my secret daily excursion down to the lake, times when I was supposed to be in the downstairs kitchen eating or in the library or even in my own room, napping. I sat, stultified by my parents' ritual of staring out the window no matter what was or was not happening outside. This habit predated television by over twenty years. That day, I knew the storm would preoccupy them. Throwing caution to the wind (who knew if we'd be asked to evacuate, and me not to be found in my room!), I slipped out and down the hall, down the stairs to a back landing I frequented for privacy and as a good vantage point to watch Renaldo's comings and goings."

The "landing," as he called it, was a ten-foot-square space directly above the stairwell. It featured a shuttered window on one side, and was completely curtained off from view by heavy drapes since no one had any use for it. Except for Gregory, who could watch the stairwell like a hawk from that position, sometimes poking his head out from the drapes, other times risking only the tiniest peek from behind them.

"Renaldo was a concept to me, the concept of true love, more than just a single human being. That's not objectification, it's deification! It's a compliment, not an insult!" Defensive, as if someone had once chided him on the subject.

I marveled at Gregory's spastic ramblings, thoroughly jealous of his hot line to elemental passion, something I could access on occasion, but never control. He told stories so thoroughly that I felt they'd happened to *me*. Whenever I think about them, or attempt to tell parts of them, I inevitably slip into Gregory's voice, and see the events through his eyes.

As Gregory told it, Renaldo was well shaped at fourteen, not the burly and solid man he would soon become—there was still softness between the muscles, a smoothness to his skin, a girlish prettiness that would soon become an almost threatening, startling Brando-beauty. If his looks—"the mile-long lashes, doelike eyes, subtle, forceful curvature of the lip" (Gregory did tend to go on)—were feminine in their prettiness, his demeanor was anything but. Renaldo was a tough kid, raised with manual labor and little supervision, a little man with his own idea of how to do things. He was capable of pushing people as firmly as he pushed boxes.

Renaldo would often walk down to the subbasement past Gregory's special landing, concealed as it was behind a propped-open door and covered by ancient, heavy drapery from the tall window. Renaldo's shoulders yawned out of sleeveless white undershirts, thighs stretching his soiled dungarees worn years past their practical limits. His eyes had an internal, almost cerebral determination, as if through all his labor, his brain were being nourished, fortifying itself against intrusion. Renaldo was a loner before the term *existed*.

Renaldo always knew when he was being watched. He would look back at Gregory, perched on the landing. Gregory would be embarrassed at having been spotted peeking at the other boy from beyond the curtains, then he'd come out from hiding as if he'd never intended to go undetected, plop down with his pale legs dangling between the brass bars encircling the landing.

Gregory's gaze was never fixed on a particular part of Renaldo's anatomy, but on Renaldo in toto. Renaldo would always stop before continuing on his way, offer Gregory a brusque nod; Gregory would feel "jolted" by the slight acknowledgment, unsure if he'd received it because it was expected as "class courtesy," or out of personal interest.

Gregory felt a strange worship for this gruff boy that he never connected to the dirty things his friends had said boys did to girls. It was like my hero worship of Andy, I realized, except I had been in the know even as a kid. Gregory put two and two together the day of the storm.

Gregory grew very still, and I felt like he and I were sharing a breath. The room fairly sizzled with Renaldo's ghost.

"I sat there on the landing, moping at the weather, pining for something—I didn't know what. Then there was an enormous commotion from beside me and I felt bowled over by a heavy weight against the door, followed by the sensation of falling as the door was jerked away from my slouching form. In my effort to make sense of the confusion, I found myself flat on the floor, staring up as Renaldo lumbered into my secret space, replacing the door to its original position and jerking the curtains around us until we were in total darkness.

" 'I knew you'd come,' he said in a loud whisper, dripping rainwater from where he stood above me. I had no idea what he meant. Had my visits to the landing been part of a particular pattern?"

That's another person Gregory reminded me of: E. M. Forster. Or rather, the character of E. M. Forster's writing, the ambience of *Maurice*.

"I felt a sickening fear grip my stomach; just being so close to him scared me to death. I struggled to right myself and Renaldo's arms locked around mine, pulling me up and into his body. Touching was not something we did in my family, and I am eternally grateful to my parents for their frigidity. Otherwise, my first encounter with physical intimacy would never have been as overwhelmingly emotional as it was. Renaldo was soaked to the bone, his bangs plastered in zigzags above his eyes. He wore only his usual undershirt, and even in the dimness, I could see his dark nipples through the thin, wet material. He pulled me close to his body and I resisted, not realizing he was doing it on purpose. Why would he want to hug me?

"He did, though. He hugged me to him awkwardly, rubbed the length of his body against me until I felt I would pass out, and then he took me. You couldn't have surprised me more if you'd told me Martians were at the door! I had no idea it was physically possible for men to *kiss*, much less have *intercourse!*" Gregory laughed loudly, recalling a naïveté from his youth that I could not, for the life of me, ever recall having had in mine. I always knew the score. In my house, if there was a *Hustler* to be found, or a *Penthouse Forum*, I would find it and commit it to memory so that my knowledge of sex of all kinds was encyclopedic by age eight.

Gregory leaned forward for impact, using his hands to tell the tale.

"He grabbed at my shirt, forcing" (fists balled up, much effort) "my hands away. He rubbed his thumbs into my nipples and I finally recovered enough to realize the enormity of the situation. I started to exclaim and squirm, but I was smothered with his tongue at my lips, in my throat. I felt he was licking my whole face, devouring my skin and then licking harder and deeper. He chewed my lips nearly until they *bled* and I felt my body respond, felt my legs ache—we were suddenly on the floor, my knees weak and pliable as he pushed them apart with his thighs. I clasped my hands around his neck and sighed into his ears as he nibbled my throat. He kissed and chewed at my chest, I groped under his wringing undershirt, grabbing at his skin. With no instruction, I reached into his pants and tugged at his penis, shocked by the alien looseness and easy elasticity at the head. It took no time at all for him to raise himself up and strip off his shirt, pull his pants to his knees—his cock was a rich, dark brown with a pink head peeking out of its foreskin, a device I'd never seen nor heard of, making it instantly exotic and desirable. I massaged his balls with the flats of my hands, working them until they shrank with excitement. He held his cock and jerked it roughly, his eyes closing, the tip of his tongue at the corner of his mouth.

"I put my hands on his hips and tugged him forward. I knew I had to eat his cock, as if tasting it would prove it was real. He straddled my face and I had second thoughts—it was sweat and several days worth of missed baths, but it was also something alluring: It was Renaldo. I ate. It wasn't the taste, after all, but the feel—the sensation of having someone's pulsing heart in your mouth.

"He sat astride my face and reared into me—I greedily licked his balls, then groaned as he roughly held my face and deliberately shoved his cock into my throat. I could not breathe—my eyes swelled as he fucked my mouth, his sighs and grunts my reward for constricting my throat to give him pleasure.

" 'You're my woman,' he said. 'I'm gonna fuck you like a woman.' Primitive, yes, but it worked for me."

We howled.

"He rolled me over and pulled my knickers aside, then worked a finger into my ass right around my shorts. I begged him to do this, moaning and sticking my butt up and bumping into the merciless finger. One finger became two, soaked in spit—I felt so desirable to command those fingers, to command the saliva he salved directly onto my asshole. When he settled on me and his cock slid in, I cried out in agony. I've never had such pain! I tried to wriggle away, but he held me with his forearm. 'No!' I cried. 'I'm begging you to stop!' He shoved his cock into me again and again and again, beyond even the pain, and told me to be quiet. After pain came the detached feeling of being part of a slick, whipcord mechanism. My asshole was his dick. I was built like a woman after all, a whore for this brute to screw at will. Even as his thrusts increased and I tried to beg for mercy again, I begged him to do it harder and harder until I knew he was pulling his cock completely out of me then ramming it back in. I came in my underpants, the spasms in sync with his thrusts. Before I'd regained my senses, I felt him spilling into me, trickling out when he backed away and slumped against the wall. He was panting, but he was immediately dressing. I stayed stock-still, my ass raised, his semen dripping from my testicles onto the rain puddle on the floor.

"He left. As he did, he knelt and caressed my rump and kissed my forehead through my wet hair. 'Again sometime,' was all he said, and he dashed through the curtains, scarcely remembering to rearrange them to shield me.

"Suddenly I had dressed and I was petrified—could not move for fear of discovery. How could such a thing occur? I wondered, stumbling upstairs and into my apartment. I'd forgotten the secrecy of my mission, and my parents had fits that I'd been out and about during a storm when they'd been sure I was snugly in bed. They punished me severely, but I can't remember how at all."

Gregory was heaving with the emotion of retelling his great

erotic moment. It reminded me of my own, but his reaction seemed exponentially more intense, if theatrical. He stared at me with his alarming little eyes and whispered, "Renaldo . . ."

Looking at Gregory, all I could think was *Andy* . . .

I shifted toward him as if on cue, ready to fuck him as only Renaldo ever had.

He seemed shocked at my advance. "No! No!" he protested firmly.

"Why?" I asked quietly, more befuddled than hurt.

"You're just horny. You don't want me half as much yet." He chuckled dryly and sprang up to clear our plates.

I AM
PATIENT

After Andrew's shocking confrontation of our feelings for each other, we sat down to discuss where things stood between us. I think Andrew had thrown my desire in my face so that he could acknowledge it and let me know that he felt the same way . . . *sort of.*

He admitted that he had never felt closer to anyone than he felt toward me, and that he could imagine living with me for the rest of our lives, but that he still wasn't 100 percent ready for the sexual part.

This was possibly the most annoying thing anyone had ever said to me. It was so beyond my control, I wanted to scream. I couldn't change my hairstyle or work out or go vegetarian, I couldn't act nicer or meaner or more convincingly; I couldn't do *anything* to *myself* to make him want me. Where's the fun in that?

"It's so *weird,*" he had said to me as we sat on the floor in the kitchen, breaking in his new kitty Judy. Andrew was all limbs sprawled out on the red linoleum, his usual sweats pulled on over my favorite underthings: bleached-white BVDs that never soiled next to his body, a sleeveless T-shirt like old men and catalog models wear. Athletic socks. He was half-propped up on the corner of the cabinet, tapping the door rhythmically with the rocking of his body. I lay flat on my stomach in a rumpled suit, sans jacket, inhaling my stale cologne that always smelled twice as good to me after a full day's dissipation. I had escorted the judge to a play. *M. Butterfly.*

"It's weird to think of actually having sex with you after all the time we've spent together without having sex," he said. "I can honestly say I love you, and that you are one of the most attractive guys I know, but . . . I don't know. I guess I have to teach my dick to pay attention to the rest of me."

I was wordless, watching the little white fur ball flop around on yesterday's news, so tiny she could hardly see straight. He'd snatched her from a litter fathered by my last cat, Malcolm. Good old Malcolm who'd never lived to see his children, who was always the only sentient being pickier than me. In a way, discovering he'd impregnated the calico next door had disappointed me. I'd always fancied Malcolm to be a gay kitty. He'd always watched me with interest when I jerked off in the mornings while Andrew was in the shower and all I could think of was wanting to be the *water.* Malcolm always purred and stretched when I came, digging his claws into my bright red shag. Yeah, old Malcolm had been into the JO scene, yet had sired kittens on the side. Maybe he'd been bisexual. Or maybe just *confused.*

"Are you listening to me? I'm trying to explain this thing."

"Yes," bitterly, while stroking the fuzzy new family member, "I am listening to every word. Tell me more."

He sighed heavily, stretched his elbows behind his back. His chest was probably as tight as Bobby Brady's asshole. Andrew gets stressed out easily.

"I have sexual feelings, but always in my head . . . I think about sex with men and it gets me excited sometimes. Sex with women doesn't excite me as much anymore. But sex with men . . . the *idea* is cool."

"But when it comes to *doing* it?"

He smiled and probably regretted it. "No dice. When I was with that first guy . . . it was too weird. I just couldn't connect that hot idea with the limp reality. The other guys I've been with . . . it's been pretty forced . . ." He cradled his face in his hands, a gesture I always mistrust because in shielding one's face, a lot more than a nose and some eyes gets covered up. What was next?

"But maybe I'm improving . . ." he mumbled.

I scratched Judy's chest and studied my prey curiously. "How?"

The room was suddenly smaller.

"Talking about all this is making me think about what . . . making love with you would be like. I've . . . got an erection right now." The hairs on the back of my neck stood up and I almost squeezed the life out of poor Judy. Lucky her, she mewed meekly and was released to streak across the horoscope.

I was going to ask him what he was willing to do about it, but on impulse, I just reached up and pressed my hand against his inner thigh, touching his warm member and feeling it pulse a little larger under my fingers. He gasped and instantly relaxed, to my surprise.

"That feels good," he whispered, finally looking at me from between his clasped fingers. The three words that motivate every human being and should be printed on our currency and incorporated into our flag: *That feels good.*

I stroked him softly for a while and he moved himself against my hands. My eyes stung, not with tears but with a flood of yearning, and I broke a sweat in my suit. Then his hands fell onto mine and he held them firmly, stopping the motion. I looked at him and knew . . . *almost, but not yet.* There was a guardedness in his expression that was fighting his efforts to open up.

I couldn't help wondering if it was the prostitution *thing.*

"I want to but . . ."

I cut him off with a calculated look of understanding, not wanting to deal with it if he was going to bring up my dates. "Don't explain any more, OK? I don't know what it's like to go through what you're going through, but it can't be fun. Don't explain any more, Andrew. Stop trying to explain and just give it more time." I tried not to sound curt. "I'll be here." *I will never give up.*

"You will? Be here?" He grasped my shoulders, the contact

making the inevitable cessation of sex all the more painful.

"Our lease isn't up until next spring, so . . ." I smiled. It was the least poisonous crack I'd made in months and we ended our conversation with a laugh, while Judy was off urinating on my jacket.

Most fags wouldn't complain. If absolutely nothing else, he loved me . . .

Something had to give.

Soon.

I AM A
CONTROL
FREAK

I went to bed, but not to sleep.

I like to masturbate. I like touching myself and feeling my body react involuntarily, the twist of a nipple making my eyes close and penis lengthen. I spend an hour before letting myself come—it's not worth it to jack off in five minutes. Being leisurely also conditions my body not to come too soon, puts me in control for when my fucking is on commission.

Jerk-jerk-jerk.

I'm fond of the feeling of my fist grinding my erection, kneading up and down in a nonstop pistoning, the sound of damp friction as a little pre-come lubricates my fingers. I lose myself in the pleasure, lock my arm into a mechanical rhythm. When I come, I always watch the absurd miracle of an erect penis, deadly still, then erupting with viscous gelatin—then the moment and the seeing and the feeling combine and I throw my head back hard and pound it against my pillow—"Yes-yes-yes-yes-yes."

Funny—"Yes," as if *permitting* the orgasm rather than acquiesing to its power.

In those seconds of unrestricted delight, I feel omnipotent that I can give myself such pleasure. Two seconds after, I feel content. Two seconds more and I'm wasted. Then I'm morose—"What does it all *mean?*"

So the orgasm is a trap, but the masturbation itself is bliss. And it's not a lonely thing, to jerk off. I don't believe that. It's not me alone, it's me with some internal lover, an image I carry in my chest of the man of my dreams—far superior to any Andrew or Andy or other derivative. I carry him inside always. If I have to die, I don't have to die alone. That's what gives me the courage to be so unblinkingly, fearlessly gay and yet so discriminating. No need to settle on a permanent partner at any cost—I'll always have "him."

My hand isn't confused over how it feels about me.

I even masturbate after a trick. (After all, that's what it is, right? Yes. Okay. Yes.) It can hurt to come again so soon after, but it cleanses.

It's an eraser.

I slept, sticky and clean.

I LONG
FOR
STRUCTURE

I was so frustrated over Andrew that my Friday work appointments following the kitchen scene had been disasters. I'd just limped through the whole act each time, concentrating on keeping it up more than keeping them happy.

The judge was most understanding. I believe he'd've been content if I just stuck any old thing in his ass and talked dirty to him. I usually really enjoyed my times with the judge if only because it never ceased to amaze me how many of his cases came up during sex. He wanted me to talk like a street kid and get lippy and pretend we were in his chambers, striking a deal. I wondered if he ever did anything like that for real, but when I'd asked him over lunch one time, he'd just winked and chewed.

The other client was so rude, he ceased to be a client. He was used to TLC and all the trimmings, and my obvious disinterest, instead of sparking concern that I may actually be *going through something in my life,* sparked belligerence and a command to "wake up." Well, that is just about where I draw the line. I was out of him and telling him off so fast, it made his ass spin. Gone were the days of my youth, when an older gen-

tleman was grateful to be able to spend time with one of the
younger set.

Whatever happened to old-fashioned gratitude? Whatever
happened to Dr. Dick?

I had never needed money after my second dental appoint-
ment with Dr. Richard Perry, D.D.S., in the summer of my fifteen-
th (!) year. "Dr. Dick" (as I called him in my mind and, later, to his
face) was a good dentist, a thorough cleaner, and not as Mister
Rogersy as most dentists are. He was a plain man with dark hair
graying in some places, quizzical hazel eyes, a rugged complexion.
He was a horse of a man, but his penis was small to average.

Not everyone can describe his dentist's penis. I can only
because for two years until I graduated high school, I had sex with
him regularly and accumulated a nice nest egg for college.

My first visit had been serene, and I'd liked his attitude. I'd
thought he must be gay then because his pants were very tight, a
sure sign if the man wearing them is not particularly built to wear
tight pants. On the second visit, I was wearing loose shorts and a
tank top. At fifteen, I was more developed than I had been with
Andy. My form was adult, if not very hairy or muscular. I now look
at pictures of me then and I can see his attraction—I was not "boy-
ish," but more like a beefy, heterosexual jock.

I was oblivious to my attractiveness, and just as oblivious to
the fact that I had molded myself to resemble Cousin Andy as
much as possible. Dr. Dick was not oblivious. He fairly shook as he
spoke to me, a change I sensed immediately, giving the sense of
impending action of some sort. He talked to me about school to a
frighteningly specific degree ("So, where in the high school is your
locker?") before asking me about sports.

I told him I hated sports and only participated in the manda-
tory gym class. Sweat shone on his brow as he inquired about gym,
about the locker room.

"Do boys still harass each other in locker rooms?" he asked,
feigning disapproval.

"What do you mean?" I asked. Alarms were going off in my
head. I'd read all about how the old ones beat around the bush,
feeling you out. I'd read *The City and the Pillar*.

"You know." (prod-prodding at my incisors in search of cavities) "The usual guy stuff like . . . snapping each other with towels . . . calling each other 'cocksucker' . . . horseplay . . ."

" 'Cocksucker?' " I asked innocently, spreading my legs a little, subtly, my self-willed erection threatening to peek out.

"Yessssss." (prod, prod) "Do boys still say things like that to each other?"

"Mmmmm . . . I don't know . . . don't *think* so." I paused, scrunching my brow, then: "I *guess* some of the guys say that."

He paused in his work, eyes burning over my crotch. His hand came to rest on my shoulder, sinking heavily, obscenely, on me.

"Because . . . there's no excuse for intimidating a young fellow for doing something every young fellow does at some point or another."

I gazed up into my dentist's eyes, eyes straining to look fatherly; desperate and afraid. Dollar signs and bells sounded at the sight of those eyes. I guess that ability to see beyond human suffering and straight into personal gain makes for a successful whore.

"Do you mean it's okay to do . . . that sexy stuff . . . with other guys?" I asked shyly. Outrageously corny! Remember, this was the eighties, not the fifties. Rock Hudson didn't get AIDS from needlepoint, and I hadn't lost my virginity two years earlier to Casper the Friendly Ghost. I was *aware* of homo-sex.

He stared down at me like an insurance salesman inches from cinching a sale. "Why, yes, yes. It *is* okay. It's perfectly natural."

His hand was sliding down some, toward my chest. I assisted, sitting up on one arm so his fingers were pinned on my erect nipple, acting as if I were unaware of the contact.

"Do *you* do things with other guys?" I asked in a wide-eyed whisper. Then, before he could reply: "Do you want to do it with *me?*"

He pressed both palms flat against my chest and rubbed my flesh through the cotton tank top, slowly, seriously. "Oh, yes—I would *love* to do it with you. I'll make you feel very good and you'll make me feel very good . . . but don't" (pause, rub) "ever" (pause, rub) "tell."

I knew all this by heart from after-school specials, except what those specials had tried to warn me against was exactly what I was looking for. I wanted to laugh aloud, but compromised with a gleeful smile incorporated seamlessly into my act. "Good! I've always wanted to be sexy with a man and I'd love to do it with *you!*"

It was payback time for all the molesters out there who'd ever taken what wasn't theirs, for free.

The good doctor was on the verge of actual tears of joy at his seemingly incredible find. His sterile white smock discarded, I was tearing at the buttons on his plaid shirt, accepting the grinding of his pelvis against mine with a chorus of moans and gasps of delight. He savored his good fortune all afternoon, canceling all appointments. Dr. Dick's good fortune became my good fortune.

I never asked him to pay. I was just about to while he was putting the finishing touches on his reassembled outfit. But he cut in, his voice suddenly conspiratorial, like the cat who swallowed the fifteen-year-old canary.

"I want you to know what we did here was a normal, natural part of life. Many men do it, average men." *Yeah, yeah, I'm here, I'm queer.* Again, I prepared to ask for money. "And," he pressed on, "I don't want you to worry that what we did is dirty or unclean." Besides sucking me off and swallowing my semen, the dentist had licked my asshole, so I was inwardly skeptical of this last declaration. Of course it was dirty . . . Wasn't that the point? "And," he said, turning to face me, hand on my shoulder, "I want you to have this."

He pressed a hundred dollars, five twenties, into my hot little hand. Where had he produced the money from? He must have had a stash among his dental tools. While I'd jerked him off, he'd shot into the little turn-your-head-and-spit sink, so hiding dirty bills among "sterile" tools was not out of the question.

"This is not payment. It's because I like you."

He never did my teeth again, though. When I saw a normal dentist in college, my teeth were fine. There was fluoride in our water, so dentists had become redundant.

I often think about those people who supposedly got AIDS from their dentists. What can I say? Mine certainly kept his rubber gloves on at all times . . . but *hey*. That early liaison in a time before I was terribly concerned about AIDS has kept my semiannual HIV test a regular adventure. I'm negative. For now.

Still, I have no regrets. Just an inexplicable fondness for Dr. Dick, corrupting angel, or rather a fondness for the period of my life before I met Andrew and the most frustrating obstacle of all time.

I don't regret any individual things. I wouldn't erase any single action I've taken. Mostly, I just mourn the fact that I am no longer a virgin in any sense. My body has been taken and has taken in every conceivable configuration. One of my clients and I used to joke that we were still virgins . . . in our *ears*. So one day he playfully put his penis into the soft shell of my ear.

Now I'm not even a virgin *there*.

I've already loved, so that's gone, too. The last holdout, the last "first," was being loved, and now with Andrew I was losing even that. It's scary. I'm never a virgin again. I can't even remember what it was like to be a virgin anymore, except how it felt to be unloved. That, I remember clearly. I didn't like it. I don't think. But I can't be sure.

Around the time of my ups and downs with Andrew, I found something out about Joe that really surprised me. Joe and I were out seeing a movie. We went to the Fine Arts Theatre, this ancient venue with high, yellow-arched ceilings, elaborately engraved fixtures, and several crowded theaters playing art-house flicks. It's a great place to see something lush and grandiose and British-seeming, just like the old theater herself. It's sort of like the Maggie Smith of cinemas, except about fifty years older.

We were seeing a group of Andy Warhol movies.

I was half-asleep but wishing I had invented The Factory myself, and Joe was bored angry, except during the film where the guy's getting blown, which he really related to, I suppose. When it (finally) ended, we sat around for a minute before leaving and Joe asked me how you write scripts for movies where nothing happens.

"Very easy," I said. "They didn't write scripts at all—that was the point, this sort of ad-libbing . . . They wanted to do away with all the precedents."

"That's scary," he said, shivering down into his seat. He was wearing his favorite tank top and pale jean shorts that tickled the tops of his knees, probably frozen solid after two hours of nonstop air conditioning. "I'd rather have some sort of foundation to go by, you know? Instead of just, just throwing it all out and starting all over again."

I think I said something like, "Whattayou know about it?" or something dismissive like that, because then he told me that he once had to start all over again and he didn't like it. I thought he meant coming out of the closet and onto the street, but he shook his head.

"No, not that—my house burned down once."

"You're kidding—the whole thing burned to the ground?"

I half turned and looked at him in profile. He nodded and a hunk of hair settled into a lazy arc to the tip of his nose. He was watching the erratic film's-end numbers on the screen, sort of lost in thought. "Mm-hm. About four years ago. It was pretty bad—we lost everything. I needed all new clothes, furniture, the works. And the worst thing I lost was my—jeez, I haven't even thought about this lately and now you've got me all—"

"What did you lose?" I prodded. This obviously had nothing to do with Andy Warhol.

"Oh, well, I used to keep a diary. I wrote an entry in it every day religiously, every day from third grade when we first got it as an assignment in school, only I kept writing in it on my own. I talked all about figuring out I was gay, doing something about it, everything. Everything that happened to me was in there. And some dumb poetry. And then I lost all my drawings—everything I ever drew in my life up until then went up in smoke. It was like—" he was straining for a comparison "—nothing. It was like nothing. Just—poof!"

I never asked him what caused the fire, sensing there was more to this terrible story. But I thought about Joe's loss for a long time. The idea of losing everything up until the moment at hand scared me. What was worse was that I couldn't think of any items I really, truly cherished . . . nothing personal like diaries (please!) or poetry (Please!) or artwork (PLEASE!). But still, how would you start over? Would you forget what you used to own, or in the case of your diaries, would you forget things you'd experienced?

In college, I once kept a phony diary for an entire month, writing as a very straight, virginal preppy boy. It was an alternate existence for me, as well as a writing exercise. For my final entry, I described, graphically, "my" rape at the hands of my frat brothers, and how much I loved it. Then I deliberately left the diary in the lost-and-found box outside the office of the campus newspaper. The next day's headline is unprintable here.

Much later, I made the mistake of telling Joe to make sure and tell his diary only good things about me, and he turned to me with that same blank-screen look and said passively, "I don't keep a diary anymore."

It made perfect sense, really, that Joe would end up living as impulsively as he was living at seventeen, having been shown the danger of relying on material nostalgia at thirteen. His only stroke of luck in the fire was that it also obliterated the bad things, the regrets.

But if, as I said, I had no precious possessions and no regrets either, what would even burn if my home went up in smoke?

I had no regrets, just complaints, and Complaint Number One was that it had taken me twenty-five years to accumulate exactly *nothing*.

Was it Dr. Dick's fault or my own? Who cares? The result was the same.

I AM
PRO-
TECTIVE

The day before the big wedding trip, I was getting ready to hit Marshall Field's for a natty new suit. What does one wear to a union of cretins? Basic navy always works, regardless of season or of the evolutionary status of the hosts.

It was late—maybe nine o'clock—but Field's was open till midnight, in the middle of its annual zany sale, and I figured I'd be the lone shopper if I went on a Friday night. That way, I could try things on without the fear of being looked at by analytical eyes, or flirted with by flamey sales clerks, who would doubtlessly have traded shifts with female co-workers rather than lose the ever-important Friday night out.

Joe emerged from the bathroom we all shared in a cloud of gay scents: soap, deodorant, toothpaste, TOO MUCH COLOGNE. Clean and whipped almost into a lather. It was that overcleanliness that made the scent so absolutely queer.

He was dressed in white jean shorts, a blue denim long-sleeved shirt with the sleeves rolled up to midforearm, a glaringly white T-shirt and matching socks rolled at the ankle, and brown loafers. His uniform was complete with a simple silver cross that swung from pec to pec as he bopped into the kitchen, moving to the beat of that one dance song they played for like a year, the one by the throaty Catholic? Can't think.

Each person may be an individual, but most individuals function as such within the confines of a larger whole. There are stereotypes, and then there are embarrassing truths. Discernible groups do exist, and members of those groups are often visually distinguishable. It's not altogether ridiculous to scout for cool lesbians by seeing who's wearing Doc Marten's, or to do a fag head count by tallying buzz cuts. Within such major groups are the smaller factions, just like how in high school everyone fell into one of about five different groups. It's *The Breakfast Club* Syndrome.

Among fags, there are several groups. Two of the largest are subgroups of barhoppers. One group is the clubkids. The clubkids wear black, accessorize themselves to shocking extremes with Jughead caps, painful rings, their mothers' makeup, platforms, gauze, dried flower arrangements, whatever. They consider themselves artists whether they've ever created anything or not, and also consider themselves too fucking cool to lift a finger to work, or to waste any of their usually largish IQs on so trivial a pursuit as thinking. Instead, they inhale anything that fits into their noses and generally try to outdo one another until one of them drops dead, after which they either reform and become boring, wasted-looking McEmployees, or push themselves until they're the next ones to buy it.

Their sister group is the partyboys. Partyboys are driven by lust, whereas clubkids just pretend to be. Partyboys wear denim, have the same middle-class sensibilities as their parents (with an aberrant taste for techno music), and have strict morals and values that entirely overlook sex, which is considered a free-for-all. They are as American as apple pie, have been known to secretly vote Republican, covet expensive cars and ranch houses in the 'burbs, and were once engaged to a woman. They, like clubkids, live in bars. They, unlike clubkids, do not fool themselves into thinking they are at the bar to have fun. They know they are at the bar to preen, to prowl, to pick something up or get picked up. The real fun will come later, and so will they, and so will the guy(s) they're with—all over the place. Partyboys drink heavily but don't do drugs, except for pot, which they don't consider a drug, and they will spend their young lives in a series of doomed three-week sex-based relationships, fucking blindly, having genital and/or rectal warts burned off, fending off straight women friends from work and calling them "fish" behind their backs, attending family functions and shrugging off suggestions that they will be the next one to get married, and working at good-paying, solid, unglamorous jobs nowhere near corporate offices, as far away from minimum wage as possible. They enjoy wearing a single gold chain for class. They grow old on barstools and drool over youthful carbon copies of themselves. They wish they were dead long before they die of natural causes at fifty.

(I'm sorry if I'm no cheerleader. I know that there are a million *wonderful* things about being gay. It's just that there are also two million *disgusting* things about being gay. But then, what's the alternative? Being straight? Asexual? Bi? Nothing impressive or desirable, or any less conflicted.)

Though I always call him a clubkid, Joe was a partyboy deluxe, with a *dash* of clubkid.

"Where are you off to?" I asked, leaning in the doorframe between kitchen and living room, watching him dance in place while pouring his third mixed drink.

"Boykultur," he replied, mangling the pronunciation. I swear, every faggot in town thought the place was called "Boypicture." Ironic that body nazis can't even fake German. Boykultur was this enormous, domed, Gothic playground complete with tiny steeples in which men fucked, one of Chicago's first New York–like *cluuuuubs*. It catered to the butch partyboys, drew enough deep-pocketed clubkids to survive, and occasionally threw a mini-bash with some tired diva and a bunch of magazine editors and managed to rake in the bucks. It was said that if you couldn't get picked up at Boykultur, you couldn't get picked up anywhere.

"I'm meeting Steven and David." (Both known to wear endearing little caps.) "There's supposed to be a lot of sailors in town. Fleet week. Wouldn't want to miss that." He laughed a little. He seemed to be done with the bathroom after three grueling hours.

"Think you're quite the little Thing, huh?" I provoked.

Joe giggled and did a raunchy shimmy as a haggard Taylor Dayne song came on his boom box. He didn't respond, he just danced by way of an answer.

"Well," I said daddily, "you just be careful around those boys. They're awfully fast, and sailors are not exactly husband material." I hated hearing myself trying to sound glib when I was actually concerned. Who was I to be so tight-assed, anyway? I was a fucking whore telling a kid not to fool around.

"Puh-*leeeez*," he laughed, bopping into his room. "I've been taking care of myself for a long time." The root of the problem.

I went into the bathroom and tore through the medicine cabinet, dislodging and cracking Joe's blow-dryer in the process— whoops! no need to tell him just then. I pulled out my electric and set up to destubble before I hit the mean streets of Chicago toward my ultimate goal of Marshall Field's. *State Street, that scuzzy street* . . . If I waited much longer, I'd have to elbow my way through the throngs of married black men cruising each other outside Woolworth's. Welcome to the third largest city in America.

"Just be careful," I called. "You act like you don't need your pal's advice anymore." *Just because I won't sleep with you, don't torture me by sleeping with everybody* but *me.* If Joe was attempting to do that, he'd end up dissatisfied anyway. I would be like that last missing, not-even-very-rare baseball card in an otherwise complete set of 792.

I never knew when Joe would take me to heart, and when he'd giggle at me and roll his eyes. This time he came up behind me while I was shaving and fell into me, hugging me to him sweetly, warmly. I tensed and he felt it, but he didn't stop, and I eventually braced my hands on the sink and relaxed, a way of returning the hug without using my arms. When Joe pulled away, I could see his reflection in the mirror, his brown cheeks, angel-grin; picture of boy, essence of man. I experienced a familiar craving for him, but it passed. I continued with my razor, and he with his last-second preparations.

Apparently he was meeting the boys to fuel up before officially going out—anyone caught dead in Boykultur before midnight and/or sober was either a fag hag or a sociologist gathering data on them.

"You *know* I need you," Joe said with a melancholic flourish, trying to appear sincere despite the fact that he already *was* and didn't need to affect it.

After more bouncing around to his party tapes, Joe breezed out the door toward Mecca.

I don't know why I couldn't get Joe out of my head suddenly. I guess my failures with Andrew and Gregory's Renaldo stories were still flooding me, and Joe just happened to be near enough to get splashed.

I later found myself across the hall, staring at his empty room. It was so youthful, a riot of all the silly things most people cherish only in their adolescence and that gay men feel free to cherish all their lives.

"What's up?"

I jumped. It was Andrew, all but perched on my shoulder. Caught! But I wasn't doing anything, was I?

Andrew looked past me and fixed on the newest addition to Joe's room, a Kewpie doll painted to look like Madonna. "Very creative boy we have with us, very . . . *creative.*"

"He *is* creative," I said defensively. "He's brilliant. He's just . . . distracted." We both knew Joe's homemade bracelets were nothing to brag about, much less buy.

Andrew looked dubious, and I felt dubious, but I also felt good defending Joe against his competition, even if I did want his competition to back me up against a wall and do me some serious damage.

"Are you about ready for the wedding?"

I said I was. I was, too. The car was all lined up, I'd packed my meager overnighter ages ago, and I was about an hour away from owning the perfect suit. I'd kept my schedule clear. I'd bought a charming ice bucket, had it professionally wrapped. I had spent two sleepless nights thinking how sickening the whole ordeal would be. Ready? Yes.

"When I return from Field's tonight, I'm all set. Now it's up to you to get me to Minnesota." He was the driver.

"And it's up to you to get me through it."

"I'll just be there as immoral support," I said, "You'll get through it yourself."

He looked weary. He'd probably had a few sleepless nights over this gala, too. "You're never 'just' there. You're not capable of being anything that's not important. You're the one who's been there for me while I vacillate over things, you're the one who's been the most supportive. Even more than my mom; at least you didn't cry when I told you I was gay." He exhaled slowly, then, "You're my rock."

So Andrew and Joe loved me for my stability. I loved Andrew for his *instability*.

I was a rock to too many people. I was sinking.

"See ya tomorrow A.M.," I replied, slinking down the hall, brushing the wall with my shoulder, staggering with a sudden sleepiness.

I AM OLD-FASHIONED

The next morning brought a sudden temperature drop and an early frost, perfect travel conditions. The trip to Hadley, Minnesota, was quite a male-bonding experience. It had all the elements of a really effective buddy movie, except the traditional implicit homosexual undercurrent had become explicit.

Andrew acted dorky on the first leg of our road trip because from his point of view, he'd done a good thing, recently confessed he loved me, let me touch It. He was behaving like a new daddy.

I, on the other hand, was extremely volatile. I'd never been so moody in my life. My victory felt particularly shallow without at least *sex*.

And then there were all these new *feelings* for Joe.

For diplomacy's sake, I tried to pretend I was just in a bad mood, but I do think he knew it was frustration setting in belatedly, after my meritorious sensitivity toward his plight in the kitchen. Aggravating matters was the cute bunny-shaped note Joe had left under my door that morning: "Have fun at the wedding in case I don't get to see you. Love." Just "love," no name. Too cute. Dangerous.

"Why do you still turn tricks?" Andrew asked me, out of the blue. Sometimes he displays a capability to say exactly the wrong thing that flusters me no end. The tone of his remark was forced objectivity. It was obvious by now that he was preoccupied with my dates. I snapped out of my daydreaming and sank down into my seat a little more, craving a doughnut and some coffee.

"Because I make a lot of money and because it's interesting," I replied reflexively. "And you know I hate the phrase 'turn tricks.' "

"Why is it interesting?"

I pressed my face against the cold glass of the window beside me, watching my breath appear on its surface. *Might as well get into this.* "I hate people, Andrew, but at the same time I'm fascinated by them. They're so *strange*. They run around so self-consciously, tending to business and spouting out morals, and then they drop the facade and indulge in this barbaric, no-holds-barred ritual . . ."

"Sex?"

I rolled my eyes. "You've heard of it?"

Five more miles elapsed before he continued his train of thought. "I guess I see what you mean." *No you don't.* "But it seems . . . weird . . . to me that you'd have sex with people just out of curiosity. Just to see them let their guard down."

"What other reason is there?"

A tentative smile brightened his unnaturally serious expression. He must have been wondering if I even remembered our encounter in the kitchen, if it had meant anything to me. *"Love?"* he shrugged.

"You've fallen right into my little trap, Andrew." I shook a reproving finger toward my driver. "Think about what you just said. If we always had sex with people we love, *you,* by your own admission, should be having sex with *me* instead of freezing your ass off on the road to this wedding."

He stiffened his arms and pressed himself back into his seat firmly, stretching. "No . . . no. That's not right. We don't have to have sex with everyone we love, but everyone we do have sex with, we should love . . . Does that make sense?"

I started to draw smiley faces in my breath on the window. "No," I grumped.

Somehow, our hands wound up clasped.

Why *did* I continue with my dates? One date in particular came, unbidden, to mind.

My least favorite regular client had been Cort, a man of forty-fivish, very, very solidly built, a redhead with a buzz cut and a rigidity that gave him away as a military man right from our first date. He was an acquaintance of my judge. An oaklike man, his social circle couldn't have been much larger than the judge, himself, and now me.

I remember Cort's initial phone call. He sounded like he'd rather be doing sit-ups than discussing his sexual preferences.

"I like to body-worship," he commented. "[The judge] informs me your body is up to snuff . . ."

"Mm-hm."

"And I'll need to be penetrated."

"In your mouth, or in your asshole?" I asked, unable to resist pushing him.

"Both," he replied, begrudging me the pleasure of hearing such a stalwart one say the word "asshole."

We'd made a date for three weeks later, the first Saturday I'd had open, but he'd called me three days before and asked me to bump him up to as soon as possible. I resent pushiness, but I was curious. I was also free that evening (if only figuratively), having just heard regrets from the judge. (I always suspected that Cort had called the judge and persuaded him to cancel.) I agreed to meet him that night.

I arrived at the hotel room first. Minutes later, I was asking him in and directing him to the sofa, sitting down opposite him in a stiff chair. I was already down to only a white robe and thongs, my hair still wet from a quick shower. Somehow, I'd known that Cort, from his precise language, would be a clean freak.

"I'm glad to see you've washed," he said plainly. "I really like a clean man."

I loosened the robe and drew one knee up to my chest, my

foot on the seat. The position was obscene—he could see my genitals and also a bit of my asshole. I was exposing myself as a reaction against his stiff reserve. "Do you really like a clean man?" I asked innocently, like I was chatting at a church social. "Do you really?"

I was aware that in light of Andrew's disapproval, I seemed to be approaching each date with newfound gusto.

Cort stood and removed his polo shirt, unsmiling, his excitement brimming beneath the outward unflappability. His chest was broad, angular, lean and firm. He had a little rust-colored chest hair, but was otherwise relatively smooth except for the shock of tangerine hair at his penis, which was unveiled when he pulled off his jeans.

It was startling to see such orange pubic hair, startling and arousing in an unwelcome way—I fought a dim memory of a naked redheaded man in the dressing room of my hometown public pool, my first sight of a mature male member.

Cort left his socks on, and also a tiny gold cross on a chain that adhered oddly to his left pec. Without introduction, he knelt and rubbed his face into my belly, licking my skin as earnestly as you'd lick ice cream. He licked and sucked my whole upper body and spent a long five minutes in each underarm. It feels good to be kissed on your body—a kiss is sweet no matter the emotions behind it, and one reserves body kissing for unadulterated pleasing. It pleased.

I never work out. I am built large, have never had to do anything to keep my muscles firm. I am not Charles Atlas, but my body has never disappointed anyone, not even the discriminating Cort, who was allowing his guard to slip with an occasional thrilled sigh.

On to the inevitable blowing. He was a good cocksucker, skilled enough to know when to pump like mad and when to draw back, lick gently, inhale, and tickle. Someone who was into Cort would've really gotten off on that. He seemed especially hot for my nuts and the moist area behind them. The clean freaks are always hot to eat ass. Sure enough, he was hungrily licking toward my asshole, which I didn't really want him to do, so I changed the subject.

"You want it in your—"

"Yes," he said, cutting me off.

"—ass?"

"Yes," he said, stealing a quick and painless taste of my hole. I stood and condomed (from the pocket of my robe) and lubed. I used the rest of my ForPlay on my condom and in his ass. He knelt on the couch, hands braced on its back, knees buried in the cushions, ass spread and arched and wriggling against my slippery fingers. I fingered him and marveled at how tight he was. I did it harder until he let a moan escape, enough to convince me he wasn't a robot after all.

I fucked him with no sentiment; he accepted me with no regrets.

He jerked himself as I screwed, and came shortly after I did.

"Never can until they do first," he mumbled as he slumped into himself, panting and dripping with sweat, come, and lube.

He excused himself and went to the bathroom. He left the door open and I understood that he wished me to watch as he used a wet washcloth to clean out his anus. He rinsed the washcloth and left it folded on the shower rod. He splashed his face, stared at himself in the mirror briefly, deeply, then returned to the sofa for his clothes.

I rearranged my robe. Ever courteous, I asked, "Was that OK?"

He looked at me and was about to say something off the cuff, but visibly reconsidered and instead offered, "It was fine. You did a fine job."

He left me an envelope with cash and I saw him to the door—he would pay for the room and I'd leave shortly afterward. We made little small talk, though I was able to learn that he had lived in at least two other cities in recent years, further proof of his secret military life. From his unfriendly, reptilian behavior, I would later wonder if maybe gays should've voted on whether to allow the military into their ranks, rather than vice versa.

As he was about to go, I exposed my penis again and told him frankly to get on his knees and suck it clean. He did so immediately, and then stood back up. I saluted him, which made his brow twitch a bit.

On a later date, he told me his last name was Marshall.

"Cort Marshall? Your name is 'Cort Marshall'? Well, I've heard worse fake names."

He offered a tight smile, devoid of mirth.

"I never believed you were a 'Cort,' anyway; I always called you 'Anthony' in my mind,"

He stumbled as he left, a rare departure from dutiful decorum, and I almost believed I'd guessed correctly.

But the main reason Cort was my least favorite client of all time was that just before my car trip to Minnesota, he had gotten very preachy on me and told me a story I couldn't shake, a story that chilled as I pressed my sweaty palm into Andrew's.

"I might have gotten AIDS from you," he said conversationally while we toweled off.

I felt my spine shake with dread. "Do you have it?" I asked too abruptly.

"No," he said, "I don't think I do. But if *you* do, we've done enough that I've put myself at risk. I haven't let you come in my mouth, but I've tasted your come. I've licked your ass. More."

"You know, if I wanted to read a pamphlet, I'd go down to the STD clinic . . ."

He pressed on. "How old am I?"

I was being kind. "Thirty-nine?"

He rolled his eyes. "I'm forty-eight. I've been living here in the city, off and on, since I was thirty-five. Before that, I lived in San Francisco. I vacationed in Key West and once went to Saugatuck. I've slept with more men than I care to—or can—remember. I fucked whenever I felt the urge to, but also had several men friends at a time. When people started getting sick—" he thought for a second "—I was stunned. I didn't know what to think. I prepared myself to be next." He was smoking, and he took a long drag before continuing. "Instead, gay cancer became GRID,

GRID became AIDS, HTLV3 became HIV became cofactors, PWA, AZT . . . to what have you. I never got sick, I never died. I've always tested negative. All of my lovers, all the boyfriends, died. They *died,*" he said imploringly, still disbelieving.

"I would hear about one, hear the impending news directly from another, find one's obituary in the newspaper, receive an 'Addressee Deceased' notice on the Christmas card of another. I even got those anonymous cards. 'Someone you have been intimate with has been diagnosed with AIDS.' They all died of AIDS, some in 1982, some in 'eighty-three, 'eighty-four . . . One just died a year ago, and another is positive but still healthy, another death I have to look forward to in the next few years or months or hours.

"I couldn't understand: Why me? Why did I stay healthy? Did I avoid AIDS because I'm superimmune? Then I did some math and realized I'd had sex—anal, rimming, blow jobs, the works—with these men just *before* they were probably infected. Albert—the one who's still alive—told me he believes he got HIV at a back-room bar he started going to in 1981, just after we broke up. I bet the next man he fucked gave him AIDS. I survived by lucking out, lucking out with a leapfrogging away from AIDS without ever realizing what I was escaping . . ." Cort was drained. He'd never intended to say so much, nor to show so much.

"I should be dead," he said with finality. Then he looked me in the eyes and said, "You should be, too."

I ended the date and refused to see him again.

When I "came to," I realized I'd been telling the Cort story to Andrew, droning it out and censoring none of it. It was as if my thoughts had been chugging forth on ticker tape straight out of my head. I don't know if I did it to test Andrew's love, to sabotage myself, or whether I did it for any manipulative purpose at all. It was the latter possibility that scared me most.

These were the first details he'd heard of my dates. The disgust on his face did battle with the compassion in his fingertips, which stroked mine sympathetically.

"Let's pull over," I said sharply, withdrawing my hand involuntarily. "I have to take a leak."

Andrew pulled into a Shell, and I crawled into its bathroom while he filled the tank of our rental with enough gas to make it the rest of the way to Hadley.

The bathroom was a regular chamber of horrors, a locker-sized, squalid hole unfit for mosquito larvae, let alone a fragile, delicate thing like myself. I locked the door behind me, breathed through my nose, and proceeded to pee in the sink. I wasn't being crass for the hell of it—the urinal was too clogged with actual crap to accept any urine. Shit in the urinal, piss in the sink, no telling *what* was in the lone toilet bowl that jutted from the wall inside a stall across from me . . . hand soap, maybe?

After I peed and washed it down with icy water from the tap marked "H," I splashed water on my face and dried off with my shirttail. Anything to avoid using the cloth toweling hanging from a dispenser like snot from a six-year-old's nose. In fact, the cleanest part of the towel looked like it was saturated with snot from a six-year-old's nose, if not spunk from a thirty-six-year-old truck driver's hose.

I'll never understand the appeal in anonymous bathroom sexual encounters. For me, it's thrilling to know *everything* about the guy you're doing, not *nothing*. And though I'm not the clean freak that Cort Marshall was, I frown on any trysting place with toadstools on the walls and smallpox virus cultivating in the wastebasket. *What kind of a sexy number would anyone expect to meet in a place like this?* Visions of Vincent Price smiling at me through a glory hole.

The mirror was clean enough to offer up a reflection, and I wasn't too damned pleased with it. I looked stoned, my eyes red-rimmed, pupils dilated. Smacking myself wouldn't make me more alert, but it might be fun to try. *Smack-smack-smack . . .*

The mating call of the rest room, I guess, because someone immediately tried to open the door, cursing in white-trashese when he discovered it was locked. Things could be worse; if I hadn't locked the door, some guy would have discovered me with my dick hanging in the sink.

I tucked myself in, zipped up, and refocused. I made myself a promise not to tell Andrew any more war stories until the issue of my work was settled—it could only lead to misunderstanding on his part, since I'd only feel the urge to tell him the least attractive tales, leaving out all the fun times and character-building experiences. Sh-yeah, *right*.

Before I left, I fidgeted with my hair and imagined myself in a wedding gown, my face a million diamond-shaped pieces behind a white silk veil. I would look fetching indeed. Perhaps even I longed to be asked that question that every girl waits to hear . . .

"C'mon, buddy!"

Enough nonsense.

I got real and unlocked the door, stepping out into breathable air. *What the fuck is that?* was my first thought, related to the hideous creature that was waiting outside to use the john.

"I'm not the one who shat in the urinal," I asserted as I streaked over to the car, desperate to make sure he knew that. Then, calling, "But I wouldn't drink from the faucet if I were you!"

We took off.

I couldn't let sleeping digs lie, so after a mile or so I snapped at Andrew. "If you think my prostitution dependency is weird, take a look at your sex phobia. What is *that*, anyway?"

Andrew rolled his eyes. I'm sure he was pissed that I'd gone from distraught to crabby.

"Well? Don't you have any clues?"

"Yes," he said defensively, "I do. I just think that sex is not something that should be bought and sold like candy bars."

"Why?"

He snorted. "Leave it to you to question something so fundamental." After a little simmering down, he said, "I don't know. I was just raised to be sexually conservative. It was like . . . I just made up my mind that sex was going to be this big, special deal when I finally had it because everyone else in school took it so lightly and they all seemed so mean about it."

What was I? *Nice?*

"And the gay thing was all caught up in that, too. Whenever I heard anything about gay guys, it was always attached to sex. *You* know that if you grew up in the seventies and eighties, you couldn't help but know about gay people, mostly from Anita

Bryant hollering about how slimy they were. Instead of just block-
ing her and her cronies out, I sort of agreed. I got defensive in my
head, thinking like, 'Not all of us are sexaholics . . . Some of us
have morals.'

"Anyway, I had this friend, or rather this *follower*, this kid
who was the son of one of my dad's friends. This guy was a couple
of years younger than me and thought I was about the coolest
thing on stilts." I looked skeptical. "No, I'm serious. I was only
fairly popular, but this guy was such a geek that I was a god to
him. It creeped me out, really. It was like too much power. And of
course, I knew I was either gay or bisexual or something fucked
up like that, and he didn't—nobody did—so it was like when
someone compliments you on something you didn't really do
yourself.

"One time we were in my car in front of his house. I was
dropping him off after a pizza party and it used to be hell to get
him out of my car—he always wanted to pump me for info on how
to be cool, get girls and stuff. We were talking about music, and for
some reason he brought up this song we'd just heard on the radio,
the one where all the profits went to AIDS?"

I nodded.

"At first I thought, *Holy shit! He's a fag, too!* but then when I
said it was cool about all the money they were raising for AIDS, he
made this pukey face and said, 'Oh really?' and was talking about
how people with AIDS deserved it because fags were just guys who
screwed around so much, they got bored and decided to try kinky
sex, sex with other guys.

"That's how that kid really, honestly thought of gay men. He
thought they were—"

"*We* were . . ." I insisted.

"—we were just perverts, just kinky guys looking to get their
rocks off in a new and unusual way. That bugged the shit out of
me, and it was the only point that kid wouldn't agree with me on.
He took every other thing I ever said and chiseled it onto two
tablets to carry down from the Mount, but he just couldn't agree
that gay guys were anything but sex deviants."

On the road, a sign: HADLEY 120.

"I didn't think of myself as a deviant. I thought of myself as normal in every other way except that when I dreamed of falling in love, it was usually with another guy, not a girl. I ended up blowing that kid off—he never forgave me and dragged my name down whenever he got the chance. He never figured out I'd dropped him because I was gay, though."

"And so . . ."

"And so, that's the thing that bugs me about prostitution. About gay guys sleeping around in general. I know straight people make like bunnies, too, but the fact is that I've always felt that since the only difference between me and a straight guy was who I was going to fall in love with, I should have all the same taboos that straight people have. Sleeping around is slutty. Being a prostitute is amoral. That's the stuff in the back of my head that I'm dealing with, OK?"

I nodded and looked out the window, convinced that this was going to be a much harder battle than I'd ever envisioned.

I remembered fondly the days before Andrew knew I loved him, and before he knew he loved me. I remembered what it had been like just to be roomies.

There was a particularly "Brady Bunch" moment once, ages ago, when I'd woken up in the middle of the night and stumbled into the living room, hoping against hope I'd make it into the kitchen for a glass of water. It was one of those nights when you start out with eighteen blankets to shield you against the sudden cold wave, but wake up to find that your radiator has overcompensated, saturating the air with dry heat.

I never made it. Instead, I found myself on hands and knees among several prostrate guys who were sprinkled around the room in sleeping bags, like a big slumber party. The two closest to me were now wide-awake, trying to figure out if I was a burglar or perhaps one of the others, indiscreetly enamored in the middle of the night. I was embarrassed to have used one of their behinds to break my fall.

"Sorry," I whispered, but I wasn't. Just pissed. "What's going on?"

"We're crashing," said one of the guys. It turned out to be

one of Andrew's Blockbuster buddies, Larry, a Goofy-like guy who always wore a "Cubbies" cap. Even, as was now apparent, to bed.

If *they* were crashing, why was I the one with the rug-burned knee?

I got up and asked, not caring how loud I was, "Why? Are you all drunk or something?"

"No," Larry groaned, "we're not drunk, we're *sleeeeeepy.*"

The other guy I'd roused started giggling and I recognized him as another of Andrew's co-workers, Terry, a flamer if ever I saw one, though he swore up and down he wasn't. He was sort of a priss and couldn't be trusted—he'd recently told Andrew that a fellow employee had lifted a workout tape, as if everyone didn't.

Now Terry was losing control, giggling and gasping for air. It's like when you have a sleep-over and you're all *really, really* tired, but you keep talking about stuff until stupid things seem hilarious, and you laugh so hard, you pee and have to disguise that fact in the morning. Not that *that* had ever happened to *me.*

I stomped into the kitchen and threw on the lights, staring painfully around at the damage as I served myself a glass of sparkling Chicago tap. Every glass we owned was sitting around, half-full of water, beer, wine, and/or soda; there were approximately nine thousand gutted bags of chips, pretzels, and (gulp) *Combos*; and five grease-soaked pizza boxes took up all the counter space and part of the floor.

Had I been drugged? How could I have slept through a pizza party going on ten feet away?

"Sorry," Andrew said, startling me. He'd crept in from the living room, rubbing his eyes and squirming in his T-shirt and jeans. "We were celebrating this raise I got authorized to give everyone and I just said they could all stay over."

I didn't like Andrew's friends. I didn't like Andrew having other friends. He spent a lot of time with these and other guys—and girls—outside of work and outside of my radar. If he didn't feel like sitting around the apartment, Andrew had unlimited resources to call on. He could always buzz Larry—one of his best friends and a rather open-minded straight guy—or Doug or Rand or Other Doug. Or Marcia, if he wasn't currently complaining about how she uses their friendship to get away with murder at work.

I don't know that I was actually jealous of Andrew's friends; I certainly wasn't jealous of that snitty closet queen Terry, who had forgotten somewhere along the line to become a man. Some of the others were okay. Larry was nice when he wasn't being a smart-aleck, and Marcia could be hysterically funny after a beer. It wasn't the people themselves I coveted, just the popularity. Or the option to do something besides work, rest, or obsess over Andrew. It would've been cool to call up my best friend, John Raging Queer, and say, "Hey, dude, let's go catch a flick." Not that I would've said anything like that, but y'know?

"I don't care," I relented, "I just don't like sharing" (YOU!) "this apartment with more than two people. At least not without some warning. I fell into Larry's ass out there."

"Maybe you've helped him with his curiosity for homosexuality." Andrew had pulled himself up onto the counter, and now stroked a make-believe goatee psychotherapeutically.

"Yes," I said, breathy like a wanton woman pretending she doesn't realize she is, "I think that brief encounter may have finally given Larry a . . . name . . . a name for that feeling he has when dropping off the kids at school, stopping at a red light, and making love to his increasingly belligerent wife . . ."

"You're insane," Andrew diagnosed. Then, laughing, "Go to bed."

Let's. "N'kay." I pointedly rinsed the glass I'd used, dried it while he watched bemusedly, and put it away. Then I sauntered past him and wove my way through the bodies—they'd all shifted position, of course—back to my room.

I remembered that minor encounter for its simplicity, and as a perfect example of how carefree things were before I'd let Andrew know how I felt, before I'd confessed it to him. But I knew I'd made the right decision to spill my guts to Andrew, then and—about Cort—now. You can end up pretty tragic after months of unrequited love if you don't come out with it, and it had taken me nearly a year.

There really hadn't ever been a choice. I mean, I couldn't have just gone on being Andrew's pal. I wasn't Larry, Terry, Marcia, or either of the Dougs. I wanted more than pizza parties and work stories, regardless of the risk. And I'd prevailed. I hadn't been rejected. Even if Andrew wasn't wild about prostitution, he seemed to be wild about me.

The remainder of the trip to Hadley was one big Dorito and Mariah Fucking Carey: We listened to American Top 40 the whole way. Everything is pretty cut-and-dried on pop radio. You love someone, set them free; love me or let me go; prove your love. It's love, or it's not love. Sex is love, love is sex. I defy you to find a Top 40 song that says, "I love you, but I'm not sure what love is really all about and sex doesn't interest me as much as blah-blah-blah." Those thoughts are harder to rhyme.

The drive had been long and our discussions had been deep and I felt thoroughly used and abused when I set foot on Hadley soil some six hours later. Talking with Andrew in that car . . . what an emotional ringer! Who expected Andrew to start saying all those sensitive, amazingly provocative things? Out of the mouths of babes.

Speaking of babes, Jill's babe was due any day, judging from her appearance. So *that* explains the last-minute invite. A lovely little mutant on the way, a nice day for a white wedding. Jill greeted us at the door to her parents' large, functional home. The building was enormous, spacious, and full of furniture so solid, it seemed indestructible, a lot like Jill's dad, Orin, the squat creature who stood behind her in the doorway.

"Hi, *Andy!*" she shouted excitedly through the screen. It was as cold as the dead of winter, yet screens were still up. I was starting to have Aunt Dell flashbacks. It was also a shock to hear Andrew called "Andy."

Apparently, all previous animosity was forgotten now that Jill was set to get hitched.

Jill threw the door open and pulled us into the living room to hug Andrew and ask all the usual questions, like "how are you," "what's new," "how's yer job." I was surprised at Jill's enthusiasm, considering how hateful she'd been toward him upon their breakup. Andrew was eating it up, too. He really needed to be forgiven for stealing that year from her life when they were engaged.

Jill was no prize. She had long, straight red-brown hair and long eyelashes, her first two noticeable features. Her face was tiny and chipper, a "real sweetheart," as she was undoubtedly called in high school: "2 good 2 be 4-gotten." She looked pretty ordinary in her wedding dress with the exception of the enlarged stomach. She wasn't a dog, though. She was mildly pretty.

Okay, fuck it: *She was a living doll!*

It killed me to envision Andrew kissing this adorable redhead, and it was no great thrill to watch him hugging her now. *How could he have slept with her and gotten engaged to her?* I tried to chitchat with her father, but the man couldn't hear a word I said over his angelic daughter's outcries.

"Got a bun in the oven," the old guy chuckled, stating the obvious. He rocked his little pickle-barrel corpus back and forth. "Can't do anything now except hope it's a boy!"

"Of course." I smiled, nodding like I knew exactly what he meant. I was fighting nausea, but was also a little amused to realize these sorts of fathers existed outside my extended family. Perhaps they are a Midwest breed. Back home, I remembered a time when a decaying great-uncle of mine had been dismayed to learn his son's wife had just given birth to their third daughter in a row, with no sons at all. "Strike three," he had chortled upon meeting his newest granddaughter.

Jill never said a word to me, perhaps intuitively guessing I was a trap-door spider or at least not her long-lost best girlfriend.

"I'm so glad you brought a friend, *Andy,*" she beamed, her eyes never leaving him. Her husband-to-be must not have been "fulfilling her needs" in those last few months of her pregnancy, because she was glued to Andrew like a stamp on an envelope. One of those stamps preprinted *on* the envelope.

Maybe she still had pent-up feelings left over from their severed engagement. Maybe . . . Andrew . . . did.

"I, uh, thought it would be okay to bring my roommate."

"I wish we could just sit around and talk for hours . . ." she said.

"Oh, she'd do it, too," her father chimed in, laughing and nudging me.

". . . but there's this little wedding-thing I have to get over with."

Andrew's smile was locked into place, tight, tighter, *tightest.* "Don't sound so excited, Jill."

Andrew! Go for the jugular!

She suddenly went dead serious and some of her beauty faded away, the teeth gone and the previously hidden excessive upper lip taking main stage with this new, solemn expression. "I love him more than I have ever loved any man in my life, Andrew."

Oh, ho! So this was her game. Lure the ex back to your wedding and rub his face in it. She must've been madly in love with Andrew.

Andrew's hands were in his pockets and his smile loosened and he seemed to be for real when he said: "I'm so happy for you, Jill."

She led us upstairs and directed us into a tiny, steam-filled bathroom to change into our decent clothes for the impending nuptials. As far as I could tell, there were no other people around the homestead. I reasoned that they had already left for the church, though the ceremony wasn't due to start for another two hours.

As soon as we were entombed in the bathroom, I went off on Jill to Andrew, snittily pointing out her obvious pregnancy and sneering at how silly it was to observe the ridiculous tradition of marriage when you aren't even observing the ridiculous tradition of not getting pregnant *before* marriage. It was like being a gay pope . . . and probably only slightly less common. I critiqued Jill's every (perfect) feature for Andrew, focusing on her only serious flaw (the lip that ate Minnesota). I told Andrew he certainly could have found a more attractive beard than Jill if he had been planning to stay in the closet by virtue of a wedding ring.

He had stripped to his underwear and turned to face *me,* the persnickety queen next to him struggling to get her jeans off. He caught me off balance and hugged me strongly, pressing into me unabashedly, just as Joe had done the night before we left. Was this it? Would I consummate my passion for Andrew in the bathroom of his ex-fiancée's parents' house? *Yessss! Nothing could be more perfect!*

I wrapped my arms around him and pressed the flesh of my fingertips into his back, savoring the slickness of his body in the steam. He was hard again, and I felt like throwing a party to celebrate it—*he's hard! he's hard!* I just wanted him to fuck me and could feel my body preparing to submit to anything his body suggested.

But even as he graced my neck with a tiny kiss, I knew it was not to be, not then. He pulled away and smiled crookedly at me.

"Just shut up," he said gently. "I know Jill's not perfect. She's not *you*, after all." I felt like a dog after a thorough brushing, all pretty and proud and "perfect." "But I'm at this wedding for *me*. Not for *you*, not for *Jill*." Devil-grin. "So just grin and bear it and maybe I'll be nice and fuck you." He laughed hysterically.

I shoved him away and finished taking off my jeans, gape-jawed with horror at his remark. What balls! "You are *not* nice." I went on dressing, scandalized. I thought I'd been hunting him down so stealthily, but once I'd told him I wanted him, he became the one in control. The hunter gets captured by the game. Not that I didn't deserve his chiding. Not that I didn't *crave* it.

Regardless of who was doing the hunting and who was being hunted, how much longer could I wait? I was dying on the vine waiting for *someone* to get a trophy.

We dressed quickly and quietly and slipped downstairs to find father and daughter at the door and ready to go. Jill seemed a little deflated, as if she realized how catty her ploy to bug Andrew had been. She looked at me for the first time, sizing me up belatedly. Perhaps she was considering a possibility that she hadn't before. I bristled.

"Isn't the wedding at six?" I asked, reasserting the fact that Andrew had not come to the wedding alone.

The father shooed us out the door. "No, it's at five now. There's a game later and we wanted to keep everyone in mind."

Jill grimaced and stepped lively out to the sedan. *"Football.* Ugh."

Andrew and I shared a smile on the way to the car.

The wedding was extravagant, an absolute spectacle of white-trash excess. The church was tiny but ornate, its wooden columns covered with more figures than there are characters in the Bible. The stained glass seemed to represent the planes of hell with every available color and very little regard for aesthetics. The pews were like kayaks, big, carved constructions with slots for Bibles and hymnals at our knees.

Hadley was a Lutheran town, don't you know. And Lutheran churches are nothing if not pleasingly vulgar. It's an extremely lax congregation that pays no attention during services attended every single Sunday. Lutherans fear God absolutely, and use Him to justify everything they do. Since I myself was raised Lutheran, I feel I have the right to do a hack-and-slash job on Lutherans in general. It's like how I can use the word "fag" and get away with it. I'm with the band.

I guess I've had a chip on my shoulder about religion ever since I heard the sermon about the Sodomites wanting to "come to know" the angel and being told what that meant and that it was just about the only unforgivable sin. If homosexuality is the sickest thing the Bible can come up with, I have no respect.

Truth be told, I was waxing nostalgic about the church. It took me back to the days before I heard that nasty sermon, when I went to Sunday school and fell asleep in the pews during regular church services and lip-synched saccharine hymns. Aunt Dell used to take me to church when my own parents got too lazy to go. Aunt Dell feared God *literally*. She was always scared to death that He would smite her or whatever. At least, she always *used* to be that way. She probably still is.

I sat next to Andrew, meeting all the heterosexual people in Minnesota and having to tell several young men, so outwardly reminiscent of my cousin Andy from so long ago, that no, I did not know the present score of the football game, but that I had heard from a reliable source that there would be a wide-screen TV at the reception if we could just make it through the darn wedding.

Andrew was nervous as "Saturday Night Live" just before the Nielsens, bracing himself for the inevitable encounters with old friends he'd shared with Jill. "I just feel so guilty," he confided, "like

I'm a fugitive that everyone's gonna spot and point at and . . . and . . . *detain.*"

"You have every right to be here," I said, "and I'm sure Jill let everyone know you were coming."

"I guess, but I'm starting to worry that maybe I'm not as confrontational as I thought. I'm glad you're here—I feel that much braver."

"Why?"

"Because there's the security that if anyone messes with me, you'll take his head off."

"I'm ready to take a few heads off right now just to relieve the tedium at this point. I can't believe you survived in this town as long as you did."

Andrew half stood up and scanned the room, but didn't recognize anyone other than Jill's family. Andrew might have had the comfort of having Mom and Dad with us, but they were sunning in Florida, and Jill had not even invited them.

When he'd plopped back down, a cricket-chirp behind us.

"Andrew?"

Andrew turned. "Candace . . . Hi . . . How are you?" This was Andrew at his least convincingly enthusiastic. Candace was a mousy girl, just a hair under five feet tall, had a sedate perm with (by local standards) tastefully elevated bangs, and wore delicate, gold-rimmed glasses with her initials screened on the bottom of the left lens. She was wearing a rose silk dress that started at her neck and ended at her wrists and ankles, like a little girl playing dress-up in Granny's old party gown. I thought she was whispering at first, but it turned out to be her natural speaking voice.

"Where is everyone?" Andrew eventually asked. "Where's Rory? And Al? And Buck?"

Buck.

"Tell the truth, I'm surprised to see *you* here, Andrew." Candace's eyes popped for effect. I wondered if she'd been voted Class Clown, or maybe Prettiest Smile. "As far as I knew, I was her only friend from Before who got invited." (Before Andrew dumped Jill, natch.) "She did a real housecleaning after you ditched, Andrew. She just blew 'em all off."

Andrew had winced at the "ditched," but seemed more rattled by the information.

"How so?"

"She said she couldn't trust 'em. She made a list of every backstabbing thing anyone ever did to her, even minor things, and crossed 'em all off her list. I was lucky she didn't count grade school or I'd be off, too."

They chuckled at a shared memory of some betrayal Candace had handed Jill in their preteens. Something involving crayon ownership.

"But why would she invite me?" Andrew asked. "I was the worst of all."

Candace relished this gossip, something that had been embargoed by the new Jill. "It's my theory that she wants to rub-your-face-in-it." She said it all in a breath, with the triumph of an amateur sleuth solving a great crime. "She wants to burn you bad." Candace didn't have much to say after that, and was probably going to be high all through the ceremony from the thrill of dishing Jill behind her back.

We turned around in the pew and sat digesting Candace's perspective, all the while making polite conversation with various strangers.

I did not tell anyone I was gay, nor did Andrew. In fact, I found my handshakes getting firmer, my voice becoming deeper, and my legs spreading when I sat instead of crossing.

"I can't do this," I whispered to Andrew when there was a lull in the introductions. "I can't believe it's come to this, but not only am I *not* going to tell people we're gay, I'm going to *go out of my way* to be as straight as possible."

He was so uncomfortable in his only suit. "I know what you mean. I was worried that Jill was figuring it out back there."

"These people would just *die*, Andrew. Or they'd just *kill*." I glanced around at the broad faces so familiar from my youth. These were the members of every football team I'd ever seen. What did I have against football, anyway? Well, they'd have never let me on their team, for one thing. And I'd almost been lynched by a football team once, just because I had defended Culture Club as good music. (I fought the good fight for Boy George before he painted that silly thing on his forehead.) Now, surrounded by guys like this as I hadn't been since high school, I made my decision easily. "We don't need to prove anything. Let's just sell out."

He nodded enthusiastically and our plan to be "out" in Hadley fizzled in a sea of self-preservation and comfort.

When everyone took their places, I finally got a good look at the groom. He could've crept down from among the gargoyles on the church's roof, as far as I was concerned. What a monster! He was the tallest man I'd seen yet, and his expression was so . . . *malicious*. He had a shaved head and kept shifting his weight from foot to foot. He pounded his best man on the back, and his smile exposed more gum than tooth. He was a *marine*.

"What a catch," I whispered to Andrew. "This could be entertaining after all." Still, Jill was going to get screwed that evening. What did I have on the agenda? "Roseanne"?

The bridal march started and I tried to remember the last time I'd heard it. It had been banned at my church while I was still worshiping with the toddlers. The minister had read somewhere that the march came from a heathen play that made fun of weddings, so out it went. The throwing of rice was also banned, on the grounds that it was a pagan fertility right. When I stopped going to church altogether just before junior high, the minister had abolished nearly every wedding tradition and couples were basically just hearing a vow or two, nodding, and trotting off, married.

Pregnant to the nines, Jill looked like heavy satire wearing white, smiling daintily on the arm of her sweating father. She was deposited into the care of the bridegroom by the apprehensive father, who dutifully took his place beside his wife, Jill's enormous mother. The mother wore a lavender caftan and her hair was extremely high on her head, wrapped around and around and secured under a tiny pillbox with a shorty veil. She was the matronly type with a large enough bosom to cradle all her blood relatives at once, presently crying her eyes out, possibly out of shame at seeing her pregnant daughter at the altar with the Creature from the Black Lagoon.

Things really got going then, the big buildup and the vows

and all. Jill's bridesmaids kept glancing out at the congregation, waving to respective boyfriends from under their lavender chiffon gowns. This was unreal—the Wedding From Hell. The groom could definitely expect cake in his face at the reception. The entire wedding party looked like it belonged on a Sally Jessy Raphael panel: Nuptial Nightmares.

As the couple exchanged vows, Andrew leaned over and whispered, "I know this is . . . tacky, but still, isn't it romantic?"

"No," I hissed.

"Just think, though, if there could be gay weddings."

"Then there would also be gay divorce."

They kissed and the crowd cheered and the rest went down in Hadley history. We stayed for the tossing of the bouquet and to see the groom's little gift for his bride: a shiny medallion that said "Death Before Dishonor." Not the most appropriate thing to bestow upon your pregnant wife, but hey, who am I to judge?

Jill was sad to see Andrew go. "Bye-bye, *Andy*. Thanks for coming . . . thanks for the gift." He hadn't brought one, but all the better if she believed he had. For my part, all I could think was: *Enjoy the ice bucket, bitch!*

"No problem," he said winningly. "I hope you guys are happy together."

She clutched her medallion and rolled her eyes up into her head. "How could we not be, *Andy?*" She kissed him a little too fully on the lips and sent us out to our rental. Bye-bye!

In spite of it all, I wished Andrew would propose to *me*. Maybe it'd happen. After all, I *did* catch the bouquet. That Misty chick had to learn it the hard way: You *snooze*, you *lose*.

I NEED LOVE

After the wedding, I nearly called Gregory on my own time just to bitch about Andrew until I realized I had come to consider Gregory a friend. If I hadn't had any lovers in ten years, I also hadn't had any friends, so that connection was almost as unsettling as when I first spotted Nervous on the bus and felt my testicles shift.

It also bothered me to be so attached to a client, but Gregory was more than just a client. He was a confidant—my *only* confidant *ever*—and a mentor. I saw my future in Gregory, saw myself in him. If Gregory and Renaldo were together forever, I could at least have a decent run with Andrew, right?

Realizing the depth of my attachment, I paced myself, swallowed my torment, and showed up at Gregory's the next Saturday morning, arriving a minute later than expected just to prove to myself I could stand waiting.

Gregory knew I was pensive for a reason, and it didn't take much insight to guess that Andrew was on my mind.

He drew close to me on the divan, laid a hand on mine the texture of wrinkled silk. I spilled my guts about the wedding, becoming evasive in describing Andrew's ambivalent overtures in his ex-girlfriend's bathroom and, previously, at home.

"You wanted him very badly," Gregory said simply.

"No," I said, stubborn to the core, "I'm just tired of adjusting to his pace. I don't want anything except progress."

"You wanted him to make love to you. No shame in that. You needed *it* and you needed *him.*"

I listened to this very quietly, my head so heavy, it nearly slumped onto Gregory's cardigan. Or onto his chest.

"Have you ever had a lover?"

"No," I replied, scared at telling so much to Gregory. "At least, not one of my own."

He laughed conspiratorially, and I had the sudden mad impulse to kiss my adopted grandfather then.

I knew that Gregory was slowly winning, getting me to want him at least half as much as he wanted me. Realizing I had not yet reached that halfway point made me appreciate just how badly Gregory must've wanted me.

We separated and I accepted an Evian and more comforting words, and even a story about Renaldo.

"I'm sure you think that since we lasted so long, we were inseparable and quite happy all the time, but not so. Renaldo was a headstrong man even at sixteen, and one whose eventual acceptance of his sexuality did not entail any acceptance of the emotion attached to it." He winced at a mothballed memory, always an enthralling, if theatrical, storyteller. "There was a period of time when he was suddenly unavailable to me. He offered excuses of prior commitments to his father, the Lake Shore, his friends. I had not even realized we'd been apart until I stopped to figure out why I felt so miserable. Three weeks that boy had stayed away from me, three weeks capped off by my confronting him in the hall as he again tried to slip unnoticed into the kitchens.

" 'Renaldo!' I scolded, suddenly fierce. 'You have been avoiding me for weeks. You cannot leave me alone so long and expect me to accept it.'

"He shoved me. 'I'm sick of you. I'm not at your call.'

"I was stunned, but I knew better than to take this at face value.

"Taking a chance, I said, 'Renaldo, you're a liar. You're just afraid to find that you cannot sleep with me without feeling towards me as a man does his lover. We *are* lovers, Renaldo.'

"I'll never know how I knew so much about love and sex, I who until then was completely in the dark on the rudimentary mechanics of lovemaking, much less the complex emotions behind the . . . thrusting.

"Renaldo stood apart from me for a long while, thinking. I could hear the cooks' laughter just below us in the kitchens, an eerie contrast to the stern face in front of me."

Gregory paused, as Renaldo had three generations ago when forced to face the inevitability of being in love with another man. I wanted to hear more, and I wasn't in the mood to feign indifference. "And?"

"And," Gregory sighed thinly like a shifting field of grasses, "Renaldo came to me that night, walked right into my room and held me tighter than I've ever been held since." He chuckled with delight. "I can still feel those arms."

"If you still feel Renaldo's body so intensely," I queried, "then why do you want mine?"

"Everyone can use a little reminder. The point is that you're like Renaldo—you both need help remembering that you have emotional needs."

When he slipped and spoke of Renaldo in the present tense, it sent shivers through me, making me wish I were an Italian boy with arms so strong they held lovers forever.

I AM
WEAK

My apartment looked like a box of crayons. I had always favored basic colors, admiring their simplicity and the irony that colors rarely exist in so pure a form. And what better place to create purity of anything than my apartment? Double irony.

I owned a lemon-yellow couch, a kelly-green dinette set, a royal-blue refrigerator, and a plum-purple rug that sat on my fire-engine-red shag carpeting. When I finally got around to renting *Dick Tracy*, I wanted to commit suicide. Why hadn't Joe ever told me our apartment looked like a silly movie set? But then, I'm sure Joe *loved* pretending he was living in *Dick Tracy*.

You've never seen such a quick remodeling job. I wish I'd never seen that movie. But you can never go back. Now my apartment is a more unique hodge-podge of startling photographic wallpaper and antique poster art. *Vive la différence.*

I also, before my *Tracy*-phobic redecorating binge, had an orange-orange jukebox full of every good song available on vinyl 45 from 1977 until 1989, when the damn things bit the dust.

Sometimes, alone, in one of my happier, more

ridiculous moods, I would open my closet with the Madonna stand-up and sing along with the jukebox to "Like a Virgin" or "Burning Up," the two best songs she ever did. The stand-up would glare at me, refusing to sing the words to the songs it knew all too well. Instead, it just watched me perform and smiled sardonically. So much for cardboard.

I pushed a button on my juke and the apartment was singing "Roxanne," pulsing loudly enough to scatter plaster on the sleeping inhabitants of the apartment beneath me. I didn't care. The husband paid me a hundred bucks every once in a while to let him lick my feet, so I knew he wouldn't let the missus complain to the landlord no matter what I did up there. I dance-stomped around a little, testing the security of my power.

Andrew had fled to the kitchen and I could hear milk pouring. He would undoubtedly emerge with a sloshing bowl of kid-oriented cereal. He was obsessed with the stuff, but he only enjoyed eating it at night. He only ate Pop-Tarts for breakfast, an entire box with a slug of OJ. What a man!

Gregory had told me I should admit to my needs. So be it.

Before he emerged from the kitchen, I quickly arranged myself on the sofa. I'd pulled out the sleeper, a perfectly natural thing to do since we often used it as an extended couch to watch movies, and then stripped to my Skivvies. Stripping was *not* a perfectly natural thing to do. I'd seen Andrew naked, but I doubted he'd ever even seen me in *shorts* aside from the quick-change in Jill's bathroom. It's not that I had anything to hide, but I do hate to show skin. It has to do with not wanting to give away too much of the game, and also to do with the fact that seeing Andrew seeing me naked would have been more (visibly) exciting than *fuck*. And overt had not seemed the way to go in bagging Andrew. Until then.

I lay in wait, my eyes growing heavy with the buzz of looking at an apartment of extreme color, and at the same time one of extreme tidiness. Visually exciting and boring at once, like MTV.

Andrew stepped into view with the bowl of cereal I'd predicted, leaning casually against the frame of the doorless doorway joining the living room with the kitchen. The trim in my apartment, unlike every other object in it, was dead white like the front door, creating an array of glaring seams staring out at you everywhere you looked. Andrew was in jeans and a Taste of Chicago T-shirt, leaning there framed beautifully, chewing, and looking at me.

He was going to fuck me silly—I just *knew* it. No more platonic.

Andrew shivered a little, and that was when I realized the apartment was rather chilly again due to our frugal landlord, Marty, Queen of Scots, the blustery Scottish female impersonator who always carried a change purse bursting with the money he saved by deep-freezing his tenants. A sneezy, pouty Judy, who was a little the worse for wear after being torn so unexpectedly from slumber by my unwelcome stroking, fussed away from me toward the end of the sofa. She was trying to get some blanket and I was trying to restrain myself from booting her off my wedding bed.

"You know," Andrew started, munching the remnants of the bowl of (Apple Jacks?) cereal, "I love you so much right now, I really want to . . . join you."

I looked over my shoulder at him, tensed every muscle in my ass, arched my back subtly. "Are you sure you're ready for this?" I had to tempt fate, had to follow through on my role as the concerned buddy.

He was smiling a little. "I won't know until I'm halfway through it, I guess. But I guess I'm ready to start out. You know. I feel like I want to do this."

He sounded so wishy-washy, I felt quick fear.

"You sound tentative."

He dispelled that worry with the firmness of his reply. "I'm not tentative about how I feel for you. I love you—I mean it."

I sank into the sofa like a cat, letting my body go limp, relaxed in the knowledge I was not Joe. I was not going to be left by the wayside.

"But there are ground rules," he said nonchalantly.

My earlier image of Andrew-as-hunter stumbled abruptly back into the open. *What was his plan?*

"What ground rules?" I asked, shifting like sand until I faced him, my body hiding under the covers.

Done with the cereal, he chewed his lip. "Nothing, really, except that you, uh, should try to curb your curiosity about men a little. A *lot.*"

I felt the blood gushing into my head, leaving it heavy and swollen. How dare he demand that I stop my dates!

Why would anyone *want* to be a prostitute, you ask? Isn't that a chore for the poor, the homeless, the drug-addicted, the self-hating? Yes, it is. But it was also the only thing I could ever imagine doing. It was more than a job, it was a way of life. It was more than a way of life, even. It *was* my life. It was *me.*

I don't know how I stumbled into prostitution. I know, I know, "Dr. Dick! Dr. Dick!" but not every kid would have taken him up on his offer. I do not know what within my psyche predisposed me to prostitution—and to having absolutely no bouts of conscience over that decision—any more than I can explain why I am gay, strong, smart, self-absorbed, lucky, you name it.

My first impression of prostitution was decidedly glamorous. Liz Taylor in *Butterfield 8.* Marlene Dietrich in *Shanghai Express.* Marlene Dietrich in almost every movie she ever made. As a kid, I felt that *call girls,* as the adults called them, were the most beautiful creatures alive (after Donny Osmond and Richard Gere, who, come to think of it, was the first male *call girl* I ever saw in a movie). Prostitutes were funny, wise-cracking, extravagant. They espoused pragmatism and looked at the world through cynical-shaded contact lenses, all the while looking like a million bucks. I felt destined to be one.

My earliest memory is of wanting to be Marlene Dietrich in a black feather boa looking up into the light, my eyes and cheekbones awash with savvy beauty. I asked my mother if that was possible and she didn't even bat an eye. "No." Well, I never ended up as Marlene, but I came as close as my circumstances allowed.

My favorite thing about movie prostitutes was the fact that if you weren't careful, if you were too busy enjoying their gloss and their sarcasm, you might miss the fact that they were always the ones with the most to say. You could always learn from a prostitute. They said the only things in the movies that really counted.

I had no concept of the sexual part of the bargain. I didn't figure out what prostitutes really *did* practically until I was *doing* it, and by then it was too late. I loved them dearly, and it was to their world I had so happily turned when the opportunity presented itself. It felt perfectly natural for me to join the ranks of all the actresses in Hollywood who'd ever played a prostitute. Every actress in Hollywood probably *has* played a prostitute at some point. So I was in good company.

It's funny—I never stopped equating my dates with movie prostitution. I was Shanghai Lily, but I was doing the nude scenes. I was living all the footage edited out from the final version.

To say I became a whore because Marlene Dietrich acted like one is facile. But I can't give you a list of reasons why I became a prostitute: "false glamour, insecurity, loneliness." You *wish.*

I can only say that I would never have become one if there weren't something inside me that had wanted me to. Do you think I'd arrange my entire life around something I didn't really want to do? And I can only tell you that whatever had gotten me started as a kid wanted to keep me going as an adult.

I became rigid at Andrew's request. "You want me to stop my dates?"

Andrew smiled and snorted. "Yeah. Is that too much to ask?" He said it jokingly, completely unaware that I wasn't about to do it.

"Do you think I just retire and collect a gold watch? It's not as easy as 'Andrew say stop, so I stop.' " I suddenly wished I were at Jill's reception with a cup of punch in each hand. This boy was absolutely tiresome!

"What are you saying? You won't stop hooking?" It was dawning on him, and he was sounding seriously annoyed.

"You don't understand," I declared, the ultimate argument, irrefutable by any opponent. Andrew was my *opponent.*

"You're sure right about that. I don't understand one bit. I don't get this. You act like you love me so much, but you expect me to carry on a relationship with someone who's sleeping with other men for money? Thanks a lot for being concerned about my health . . ."

I didn't know what his game was, but it was working. I blew. "Don't you even *fucking* try to tell me about *AIDS,* little boy! *AIDS* is not the main issue here. It isn't even an issue, period. You know damn well how safe I am on my dates and you know damn well that I would have safe sex with you the whole time and you also know that either one of us could already *have* it and not know anyway . . ."

He blew. "What a ridiculous batch of excuses! Like there's such a thing as *safe* sex! Like having sex with multiple partners doesn't increase the odds of getting it! Like you're *really* always safe!"

"Like *shut the fuck up, Andrew.*"

The bell sounded and we both shut up, stewing in our own frustration and anger at having had our first shouting match. My defensiveness shocked me. *Where the fuck are my clothes?*

There really was something to this prostitution thing that made me ill at the mere suggestion I give it up. Instead, I was ready to give up Andrew, whom until that moment I had been touting as my personal sexual savior, and the man I wanted to "settle down with." Had a year of my life gone down the tubes? Or had *ten* years?

"Look." Andrew sounded a thousand years old when he broke the frigid silence. I felt *two* thousand years old. "I just think you're being selfish to risk our health."

He was more fixated on a monogamous relationship than I was on prostitution.

I was less bombastic than before, but still ruthless. *"Your* health, Andrew. If you gave a fuck about *my* health, you'd have expressed your concern for my safety sooner. After all, I've been going on dates for the whole damn time you've lived here." When that had sunk in, "The point is that this is not an argument about AIDS. If there were no such thing as AIDS—"

"Or syphilis, or genital warts, or herpes—"

"Or whooping cough," I curtly interrupted. "If STDs were nonexistent, you'd still be asking me to give up my dates."

Andrew snorted again. "There you go with 'dates' again. Now I know what my mother meant when she said she didn't want me to 'date' until I was sixteen. *Date me, date me!"*

"Date off, Andrew. Just listen to me, OK? Can you listen to me?"

Grimly, "Say something worth listening to."

I just wanted to die as it all hit me, watching his handsome, crooked face twisted with concern. He looked like a man who'd lost everything in about two hours, and he probably had. His sexuality was about as stable as Connie Francis, and when he'd finally made up his mind about a relationship with me, I'd turned into a militant prostitute.

I was at wits' end. At that point, I'd've turned cartwheels to get him into me, but I wouldn't promise to drop the dates. It was the principle of the thing. How could I possibly admit I'd wasted a decade of my life? Maybe it was my turn to need time before green-lighting anything.

"OK, you win. I won't call them dates anymore. I don't know why I ever started calling them dates in the first place. To be funny, I guess."

He sighed. "That's your problem. You're always funny. You're too funny for your own good. You wonder why I don't always listen to you. It's because sometimes I *don't feel like laughing.*"

OUCH.

I wanted to make a joke to pass off some of the sting, but realized if I said anything funny in the next twenty minutes, I'd be proving his point all the more.

"Let your guard down, goddammit, let your fucking guard down."

I stared him down, broken. The next thing I said took all the guts I had and made me feel like shit just saying it. "I *can't.*"

"Why?"

I closed my eyes and tried to say what really came to mind before I could think of a convenient response. "Because if I do, someone will . . . take advantage of me." I wished I could take that back as soon as I'd said it, too raw, too real. I made a concerted effort at resilience. "Why are you bringing all of this up now?"

"Now's the time. Now or never."

"You're right. I know," I conceded, feigning heartfelt agony, telling myself I was only feigning it. I cast my lashes downward and produced a single tear. I was practically crying for real at that point, out of sheer exhaustion. *Date me, date me.*

"I know I'm never serious. I can't help it. I think I don't make sense if I don't make jokes. But still, you know *I'm* right, too. You think prostitution is really, really *dirty,* don't you? It's not just the fear of diseases or the jealousy of me being with another guy, is it? It's the thought that I'm dirty. That *I'm* morally dirty. You can't get over your upbringing."

"*You're* saying that, not me," he said. Then, with more conviction: "Yes, OK, you're right. I think prostitution is . . . *gross.*"

His choice of words was so funny, I started to laugh nervously. That got him going and we dissolved into hysterics.

"So that's the bottom line, hey? I'm 'gross.' "

"No." He bounced a hip against the frame rhythmically. "That's the thing. *You're* not gross. But prostitution is gross. I have a hard time connecting the two—you and it. I guess I almost disbelieve that you actually do the things you described to me . . . all that stuff you said you did with that Cort guy . . ."

"I never lie, Andrew. I do it all."

"Why?"

There may as well have been a spotlight; me all alone there on the sofa bed. I still wasn't prepared to do my autobiography just yet.

"If I knew the answer to that, maybe I wouldn't have to be so funny all the time. Why did *you* spend a year of your life pretending you were straight to please Jill?" I looked at him quite sincerely, and saw the poignance of my remark register on his face. Then, softly: "*Please* . . . don't just tell me to stop it. Your *telling* me to stop it just makes it harder to want to. But I do want to be with you all the time . . ."

"You can't have your cake and eat it, too."

"Why not? Whoever made up that rule was born bitter."

There was no way I was going to lie to Andrew, tell him I'd quit prostitution for good, get fucked, then go right back to dating the next day. No, despite the urgency of my need, I was wise enough to think ahead. I wanted Andrew more than just once. I had plans for that boy. I wanted him as a live-in. If that meant giving up prostitution, it meant giving it up for real. And more than any other thought I'd ever had, it scared the shit out of me. It was like an artist contemplating the destruction of all his paintings in order to start afresh. Or like Joe, contemplating the ashes that had been his diaries.

As if on cue, I had this strange surge of feeling for Joe. Joe, whom I'd been so quick to dismiss. Joe, the safe option. I was mad about Andrew, but Joe's hug lingered in my memory alongside Andrew's. I dismissed it and focused on Andrew.

You'll think me shallow, and I swear to God I was in love, but more pressing was: *I just have to get fucked, I just have to get fucked* . . . Do you understand that feeling? Like silly freshman girls who just *have* to lose their virginity, except I just *had* to lose mine *again* . . . And then what?

Defeated, Andrew shrugged, left his cereal bowl still half-full of sugar-milk for the nimble Judy, and shrank away to his room to sleep. I doubted I'd ever have another erection as long as I lived.

I AM
PETTY

I am, as you may have gathered, a touch antisocial. I am also a little put off by some of my peers, am not looking for quick sex or even to add to my stable of clients. So you would probably wonder why I was sitting in a gay bar about two hours after my showdown with Andrew.

Dicks (note the lack of an apostrophe) was the only gay bar I'd ever been in twice. It was an old shoe to me, a comfy slipper. Instead of the usual grungy bar full of ancient leathermen (I'll never forgive Al Pacino for making me so afraid of leathermen), or the usual (snap) *cluuuuub* with strict admissions policies and more back room than front room, Dicks was this nice, energetic little bar full of preppy types, average guys, your next-door neighbor, that gay Uncle Artie you kids always liked so well. Everybody simply had "a beer," and if they felt like dancing, there was an unpretentious little dance floor with good enough lighting to look for Mr. Right and yet enough shadow to take a year or two off the old keister.

What did I do at Dicks? Thought, mostly. I sat and drank an Evian at a small table on a stool with only one empty stool next to me, which I always covered with my jacket so no one would think I was free and seize the opportunity to sit down.

I liked to see who was gay as of late, how gay guys were acting, what they thought was presentable and mildly hip to wear when out meeting men. There wasn't a lot of cigarette smoke in the bar, either, and absolutely no marijuana, and no underaged slicksters in Italian suits trying to unload some Ecstasy or coke on me. REM was played every third song, right after a Donna Summer classic and whatever was at number one that week. In short, Dicks was a place I could go be gay without any distracting extras.

That night I was thinking about Andrew's concerns over my prostitution, and about my own thoughts on the matter. Was Andrew going to be worth such a major change? I would be giving up a lot, but what was *he* giving up? Celibacy?

But that was the kind of tit-for-tat mentality I had to lose. In prostitution, every action is contingent upon a dollar amount. A hundred bucks: you lick me anywhere. Two: you can suck my dick. Five: I'll fuck you. I did things for money.

With Andrew, I would be doing things—both sexual and not—not just because *he* wanted me to, but because *we* wanted to. I couldn't weigh Andrew's merits pragmatically and decide based on that. I had to consider first that I was in love with the guy and that I wanted him more than anything else in the world. Almost.

I sipped.

Around me, the dance of the pigeons was going on. You've seen pigeons going at it in the park? The boy pigeon's feathers get all poofy as he struts around the girl pigeon, who agilely maintains perpetual motion until he traps her and jumps on her, fucking like crazy for about a minute. Try to imagine how it'd work for two boy pigeons: both poofed up, strutting like crazy, attempting to jump on each other, fucking for a minute straight . . . That's what Dicks looked like.

All the boys were running between loose circles of guys in polo shirts and long shorts (*lots of nice legs tonight*). It's cute to watch sometimes, but I don't understand why guys are so willing to fuck around. It seems to devalue your body to pass it around so freely, you know? I mean, I have a lot of sex, but none unless I'm being paid for it. Some guys would think that's the lowest of low, but isn't it better than thinking so little of yourself that you'd spread for any operator with a smile and a wink and a room for the night?

I guess it all comes down to pleasure. If you're getting pleasure from it, it must be worthwhile. My question is: Do all these sleep-arounds actually get that much pleasure from all of their encounters? It unnerves me to consider such a thought because I don't think I'm physically capable of *really* getting off with so many different guys. Am I selective? Prudish? Dysfunctional?

Too, there is so much energy invested in cruising. Think of all the time spent working out to get in shape, developing an attractive style, learning to be charming, getting dressed, sitting around in the bar attempting to meet partners, drinking, chitchatting. You get laid. You never hear from the bum again. You invest all your energies into cruising again, sure that the next guy you get will be a prince. If gay guys stopped spending so much energy barhopping, think of all the da Vincis we'd have emerging from the gay ghetto in the nineties. Think of all the Schuberts, Nijinskys. Instead, we have a few million *really* great-looking guys with steady jobs and full dance cards. And me.

"Hey, you mind if I join you?" It wasn't da Vinci. The guy deposited my jacket on my lap, his hand brushing my leg, and sat down on the verboten stool next to me. He was tall, blond, suburban, little mustache, slim but probably a recent inductee into the faith of bodybuilding. He had a nerdy face and his big body seemed ill suited to him, a basically yucky guy who'd improved his odds by getting a body. Sometimes, looking around at my gay peers, I felt like Donald Sutherland in *Invasion of the Body Snatchers,* except bodies weren't being snatched, they were being enhanced.

He was smiling forcefully between slugs of a Miller Lite. He'd had no intention of waiting for me to invite him to have a seat, so I had no intention of letting him leave the table with his balls intact.

I glanced up with a look of such malignance, he almost fell

down. Then he regained his composure and plunged ahead.

"You look lost in thought over here." (guzzle/grin/guzzle/grin)

"No," I replied. "I'm just trying to have a moment alone." (sip-sip) *No dice.*

"Well, you shouldn't spend so much time alone. You're too cute not to share yourself a little bit."

"I failed sharing in kindergarten." *God, everybody wants a piece of me. Leave me alone.*

(Guzzle/grin/guzzle/grin) "You're really funny. I can tell you're used to guys pestering you. But I'm not looking for anything sleazy. I promise. I'm just thinking you might want to go get something to eat with me." *Push-y!* Something to eat. Like his dick, maybe.

I studied his face closely. But no, there really wasn't anything . . . "What exactly do you think makes you so hot?" I asked dryly. "What do you think you have that a million other guys just like you *don't?*"

It dawned on him that I wasn't playing hard to get, and that his come-on wasn't getting me hard. In fact, I'd just said something remarkably rude to him. Castrating, even.

His comeback: "So what makes *you* so hot?" He was pissed.

(Guzzle/grin/guzzle/grin) Copying his style was the coup de grâce. "I don't know. Why don't *you* tell *me?*"

He turned tail and took off, muttering something about "asshole" and "games." Am I a games player? I ask you: Did I flirt with him, tease him, *lead him on?* Let him go fuck his girlfriend. *Farewell, Mr. Guzzlegrin. We'll always have Dicks.*

So much for peace and quiet. I finished my water and made my way through the crowds toward the front door. On my way, I saw Mr. Guzzlegrin one last time. He was pointing to me and talking about me to his friend, a cute, red-faced, collegiate Asian with swollen biceps and bee-stung lips. When both were looking at me, I gave Mr. Collegiate the most alluring look I could summon and mouthed as clear as can be "I want you" just before I slipped out the door.

Now, *that,* class, is games playing.

I NEED
PEOPLE

CONFESSION 16

Sitting around with Gregory, I never expected it when the time actually came. *Consummation.* The word is rich with sex, isn't it? If I close my eyes and say the word, I see little flowers in bunches, slowly igniting as a spirit-quick brushfire dances over them. In a second, they go from thread to flame to smoke, *consumed.* I think real passion is like that. True, it's often a long, laborious buildup, but the actual moment when something is going to happen is like burning flowers—one minute your mind has a delicate, deliberate thought pattern like the structure of a flower. Then you lock eyes with another human being and your mind disintegrates: flesh to fire to smoke. It's inescapable, and irretrievable. That's why losing your virginity is such a big deal. You're not simply doing something for the first time, you're evaporating and continuing life as a whole and different reconstituted element.

For the time being, I was blissfully unconcerned about when or if I'd ever have sex with Gregory, having decided long before that he'd never believe I was hot enough for him. I was lying back on his sofa, my arms over my head and dangling from the armrest, my bare feet propped on the opposite armrest, a foot away from Gregory, who was alternately reading the *Trib* aloud ("Bette Davis is dead! I can't believe it! This proves she was actually *alive* those last few years." In truth, he was inconsolable over this loss.) and sipping brandy from the most mannered little goblet I'd ever seen.

"I'm so worried about Joe," I muttered, surprising myself. I'd actually been mulling over my spat and war of silence with Andrew. Or had I?

"From what you've said," Gregory intoned, "I must say he seems to be perfectly fine. He sounds like a young boy sowing some oats. Granted, he's had the bad luck to be thrown out of his parents' home and so he's sowing oats a few years earlier than most of the rest of the *boys*." (I always suspected that Gregory resented gay youth in the nineties for taking for granted their relative freedom.) "You're not so much worried about *him* as you are worried about your *feelings* for him."

I chewed on that for a while. It was probably true. I needed Joe because he, like Gregory, was one of my only friends. I needed Andrew because, well, it's like how he called me his "rock." He needed to hold on to me, and I needed to be held.

I had done such an excellent job of divorcing myself from emotional attachments for so many years, it was overwhelming to suddenly need Andrew *and* Joe, albeit in different ways, both at once.

The first divorce had been the hardest, but also the foundation upon which I built many divorces to follow. I bet most queers have to make this divorce, though admittedly (and here I am a little envious), more and more do not: I had to lose the parents.

Like every good little faggot, I once loved my daddy and was attached to my mommy at the hip. In my childhood, Mommy was so *pretty*, with the long blond natural hair of the early seventies, but the sense of style of a cute wifey—a throwback to her formative years in the fifties. She didn't work; there was no question. My father didn't forbid her, it just never came up. She had never, ever worked a day in her life. She simply took money from her parents until she met her husband, and then took money from him. She's the kind of princess whom people can't resist, and so she never had to question where her next meal was coming from. Mommy doted on me, asking me more than once, her saucily flared little nose poised just above mine, "How'd you get so *pretty?* Who made you such a *pretty* boy?" The unspoken answer was, of course, that *Mommy* had. Forget about God—Mommy was an atheist, too stuck on herself to look up for inspiration. And forget about Daddy, who, despite being sexy and rather classically handsome, was physically unidentifiable as my biological father. My dark hair with renegade blond strands is my single Daddy-like feature.

I adored my mother. She never left my side, always show-ered me with toys—I never had to beg for any prize. When Earth-quake Tower came out, I had it within the week. I had Green Slime before anyone, a Rubik's Cube, and generations of Slinkies (those things last about as long as hamsters). Mommy gave me everything except any semblance of true warmth. *Sob.*

Daddy. My heart used to thump whenever I so much as thought of him, right up until the day he caught me masturbating. This was way, way after the Mommy-and-Me years, when I was too old to cuddle, too much a competitor for attention, when I was twelve, not terribly long before my legs would be locked over my cousin's brawny shoulders. Though I knew everything about sex early on, I had only recently mastered the art of teasing come out of myself, and spent long hours perfecting the technique in the soli-tude of my room, snugly hidden in my closet so I could pull up my shorts if I heard anyone enter.

The day I got caught, I was looking through a menswear cat-alog, probably Sears, and also at a small cache of Lorenzo Lamas photos I'd stashed (okay, so sue me—my taste has improved in the last dozen or so years). I never fantasized much about real sex, just about men looking directly into my eyes and holding my hand and stroking my hair. Stroking my hair! I blush at the thought, how-ever innocent, because for the first time, as I write this, I am con-fessing my most intimate erotic turn-on from that part of my life. I still love to be stroked.

There was never a sound, which told me that my father had deliberately snuck in—my bedroom door was a loud muthafucka, a big old wooden ordeal with hinges as cackly as your dead Aunt

So-and-So. With no preamble, my closet door was just suddenly, silently open, and I stared up into my father's deadly glare as I shot spunk all over page thirty-eight, Underwear for Him.

"Look what you've done," my father said, his voice crackling with a parched rage. He stared at me and I drew my knees up to my chest and fumbled with hiding the magazine.

My father had always been a bastard, hence his eventual slide into small-town politics. First and foremost, he was a coach. A minor leagues football coach, nothing more manly to be, except maybe a Green Beret, which you can't do when you dodge the draft at a second-rate junior college a hop, skip, and a jump away from the Canadian border. He was hot, I will admit, a GI Joe doll with a then fashionable butcher-than-that mustache. He was much-beloved by his players, mostly black, who never knew—but probably guessed, if their street smarts were working at all—how much he loathed their race. My father won many a local election on 80 percent black votes, all the while bitching to his family about the jive-ass turkeys he hated to have to coach. He would gripe about them to the point of throwing a temper tantrum, pissed about having heard them bragging about screwing a white girl, then calm down and be so charming, my mother would invite the neighbors over to show him off. He had a beautiful body, fleshly, not the Teflon builds I see today hanging out of gay bars. He had a hairy chest and enormous hands and I even remember seeing him naked as we showered together when I was younger than five. I remember naïvely touching his penis and asking what it was and why mine was different, and he had the uncharacteristic good grace to laugh it off, gently push my fingers away, and say, "You don't want to touch that. But it's called a" (whispering) *"penis."*

My childhood was a series of near-fatal rejections from my father. I was built for sports and could run faster than lightning, but had performance anxiety and couldn't be bribed to play. Nonetheless, I was signed up for every youth sports team in the Tri-City area, and forced to live an excoriating existence of steadfastly refusing to participate, making me the ultimate enemy of every little boy in the world: the big, fat sissy. I pitied my sisters since they were ignored even more blatantly than me, but even they looked down on me as a Brucie Boy.

By age eight, I had figured out exactly why I was different. I had seen pictures of boys touching each other's *penises* in all the elaborate pornography my friend (Jake? Jack?) showed me in his older brother's groovy love-van. I absorbed one image after another, mostly of men barely touching each other as opposed to the guys on other pages who were all hands-on, gang-banging some stringy-haired girl. The men weren't anything great themselves, skinny, pallid, you just *knew* they smelled of incense and didn't believe in deodorant. But I craved their touch. I wanted to grow up overnight and be able to touch some man's *penis*.

If I knew I was a *penis*-toucher as opposed to a gang-banger, I also knew I had to keep quiet about it. How do kids know this? Few parents actually say: "Here's what being gay is. Now, *don't do it.*" Instead, there is a subliminal cultural law out there that told me to keep quiet about *penises* until I found someone who looked like he was keeping quiet, too.

After eight, I remember only a few scenes from childhood leading up to the day my dad watched me come, at twelve:

• waiting anxiously for half an hour, forty-five minutes on the curb . . . my father was late to pick me up . . . I was always hanging . . .
• my hair too long and my father too busy and my mother too self- and/or house-absorbed to cut it . . . being asked by an older kid if I was a boy or a girl . . .
• killing bugs compulsively and then lying to my mother about it when she questioned the kooky little wooden crosses (made of Popsicle sticks) I'd erected in the garden . . . I was a Goebbels to the bumblebee . . .
• first sticking my finger into my butthole, feeling like I had invented kink . . .
• an episode of "Real People" featuring drag queens, watching in fascination their enormous, *real* breasts, agog at my mother's pursed-lip explanation of how they got them . . . they went to the doctor and simply *changed* their bodies . . .

• catching two of my dad's favorite players kissing in the same way Daddy kissed Mommy . . . *are they like me?*
• getting in trouble with my aunt for having doodled naked girls . . . she never found the naked boys, tucked into my tiny pockets . . .
• saying the word "nigger" aloud at a football game, my good-hearted babysitter shushing me . . . realizing the word my parents used so frequently was a foul slur . . . hating them for tricking me into using it . . .
• being endlessly entertained by building blocks and little plastic animals way after other kids my age went for more exotic amusements, like video games and watching the Play-boy Channel on the sly by forcing a playing card into the cable box . . .

Most of all, I remember being relatively happy in my childhood, pitying various friends whose parents dropped dead, who were so dumb school seemed like a form of torture, who were too poor to eat hot lunch, who wore glasses, braces, or rode in preelectric wheelchairs. I remember feeling I was the only normal kid, then would feel queasy remembering I was, after all, a *penis*-toucher.

I was a solitary animal. I lived in my room. Period. I got fat, drank more Coca-Cola than you drink water, read every book ever bound, and wrote little stories about sophisticated murder and wild romance (boy-girl). My mother was at first concerned, then embarrassed, then gave up, and never much spoke to me or about me as she became swept up in PTA drives, neighborhood watches, the occasional (yes!) Tupperware party. When she discovered Mary Kay, it was like she was born-again, and her face, quite literally, *was*. Unfortunately, the new face—slathered with foundation that ended with a snap at her jawline, eyes kohled, lips glistening with purplish goo and shellaked with gloss—was more afterbirth than rebirth, and her draglike transformation made it that much easier for me to inch away from her.

My mother? I loved her. My father? I adored him, worshiped him, wished I could be as beautiful as him, as strong; at times, even desired him, for lack of anything more perverse to imagine. Not really, though, just one of those Freudian things, an urge I would later reflect on in disbelief.

But all of these emotions are in the past, because as I started to say a long, long time ago, I have divorced myself from them.

I doubted my father realized I had been jerking to pictures of men, but as he stared down at me and I scrambled to pull my pants up, I decided to transform. If Mom could do it, if drag queens did it, then I could do it. My mother was useless, my father was dispassionate and brimming with undirected hatred. To hell with them.

"What the fuck are you doing sneaking into my room? Get out of here or I'll KILL you!"

My father went ashen, opened his mouth, then turned away and slammed my door.

I sat there for about thirty minutes, aching from the hostility, my throat tickling with the stress of having screamed at the top of my lungs. My come was drying by the time I tore out the soiled pages and wadded them up, dabbed some off me with my dirty sock, pulled my pants the rest of the way up, and stumbled over to my bed. In the space of two minutes, stretched over the first twelve years of my life, I had dropped my parents like a pair of pants. From that day on, I never gave one single, solitary damn about them. There was an unspoken understanding between me and my father: We were no longer father and son, but we would keep up appearances. I used them for food and shelter all the way through high school. Then I left them. I was determined not to rely on them for college, or for anything else. After years of playing it cool to eat well, I was ready to strike out on my own.

I think this sort of ruthless pragmatism is the rule of the day for fags, the bravest of us, anyway. It may seem cold to put self-preservation before family love, but only if you've never doubted it when your parents said, "I love you—no matter what." When there are limits to love and you're twelve years old, you start wondering how you would survive if you were dumped onto the streets. Keeping that in mind for the next six years before you graduate high school (assuming you make it) can milk a lot of hatred from an otherwise loving individual. And it can make you practical to a fault.

I was never thrown out of the house because I was gay. Instead, I was emotionally starved, all (I am convinced) because some part of my parents' brains told them I wasn't "right." I divorced myself from them because some part of my brain told me I was gay and was going to be automatically rejected for it.

Today, my parents have no idea where I live, unless they've looked me up in the phone book. They know I'm gay only because the rest of my hometown finally told them. I hope I never see them again, and I wish them deaths as painful as the death they gave me when I was little, going from innocent love to the worst kind of betrayal any person can ever commit against another.

I left them in the dust because of their unspoken distaste for me. The whole issue was decided wordlessly. We never spoke about it, and now we'll never speak again. And that has nothing to do with my "choosing a lifestyle" or "the way they are, they can't change." It has to do with the fact that I had the bad luck to be born to two of the coldest motherfuckers who ever climbed on top of each other and made a baby.

As Gregory sipped his brandy, my head was reeling, mulling over emotional divorces: parents and family first, then Andy, then a string of unworthy friends, then anyone I ever found vaguely attractive. Lately, though, I'd been letting a few people slip between the cracks. Maybe Andrew was so important to me because I had actually advertised for him, had hand-picked him to enter my life. Maybe this whole divorcing thing was really about rejecting people I never had the option to accept or reject, people fate threw on me. If so, "divorce" is a misnomer in my case; you can't divorce someone you never married in the first place.

I snapped out of it and my eyes focused on Gregory's. He was staring at me furtively, looking distracted even though he was unblinkingly searching my face. My friend, and I loved him for that.

Now or never.

I got up. I went over. I kissed him—he sighed like a sheet of paper slipping under a door. I kissed directively, moving his head with my mouth. He kissed leisurely, like we had all the time in the world, or like he was savoring something delicious and rare. Gregory's head rested in the crook of my neck, his fingers nimbly unbuttoning my shirt, pulling it open. *He smells of pine,* I remember thinking. His nails traced infinitesimal circles around my pecs, brusing past nipples firm and inflamed. I've never experienced such attentive and exciting worship of my flesh as I did with Gregory. He covered my chest with more kisses than I'd ever received on my lips in a lifetime of professional intimacy.

When he blew me, I closed my eyes and saw him as a blond wag, hardly sixteen and already mad over Renaldo the dark-skinned godling. As he lavished my testicles with an unwithered tongue, I opened my eyes and saw him as he was, a handsome old man, firm of jaw and flushed with passion, his hair still soft if white with life. I guided him back to my penis and our eyes met before he went down on me; we looked at my erection and marveled at it, both equally impressed, not with my size (please!), but with the shape of a human penis, the superstructure, the red vigor, the tender buds of skin at its peak where a mouth of any age can trigger a pleasure so fine it's agony. This erection had been our project from the time we first met.

Soon enough, he was back in my arms, bringing with him the scent of his perspiration. We got naked and very serious and it seemed natural when I turned him around to hold him to me in a venal fetal embrace. I couldn't stop running my hands over his papery skin, over the dark spots at his forearms that, despite their severe appearance, were unfeelable—all talk. His ass was cuddled into my groin and felt warm and dry and soft—not unlike the other men's I'd been with, but worlds apart from the cultivated, muscular buttocks preferred by most men my age, whom I'd never slept with. He reached back and held my penis firmly, his thumb smearing my pre-come over the head. He suddenly hopped away for a moment to retrieve a condom from his nightstand and a new bottle of ForPlay from beside his bed. It was weird to see such an old guy hauling out his ForPlay, but I guess that's how you survive in the world for eighty years—you adapt.

I asked Gregory to put the condom on me, which he did, then asked him to smear lubrication on it, which he did. We lay down on our sides on the bed, and I squeezed a palmful of lube into my own hand and flattened it between his soft ass cheeks, running it over and just into his anus—he moaned—and we resumed our fetal hug. He ground himself back into my fingers and lifted his leg slightly, with effort. I assisted by placing my fist between his thighs to help open him for me, then I slowly, and not without three serious, failed efforts, worked my penis into him.

I've never fucked so slowly, nor so single-mindedly. I know I never stopped in my simple to-and-fro rhythm, except toward the end when I screwed him more desperately in a slight circular motion, rubbing myself in that last extra way to help me come as intensely as I felt I should. I wanted to give it up but *good* for my pal. I shivered, admitting to myself that if Gregory weren't paying me, I'd still be doing exactly what I was doing.

Gregory reached back and grasped my forearm, stony with determination, and gasped that I was "so strong, so strong," squeezing me tightly from inside. I finally withdrew my cock completely, then plunged back in, and he seemed to collapse in exhaustion. But that last gesture was all it took and I came, loudly and at length . . .

. . . I let my hand drop over his body and felt that he'd had an orgasm at some point, though I didn't know when. I ran my fingers through his still vital seed, imagining I could feel it slithering with life. We breathed deeply and in tandem, never spoke. We slept until dawn and rose to the sounds of college students behaving like schoolchildren outside Gregory's door, then reengaged. This time I took him in my mouth, drinking until there was no more to be had.

I felt like I hoped *Andrew* would feel just after making love to *me,* totally connected. It was like foreshadowing. It was like an appetizer. It was, like, the first sense of intimate connection I'd had since I'd been on the receiving end of the thrusts a long time before.

It was also the first true pleasure I'd allowed myself in years. So I freaked out.

I AM PROUD TO BE GAY

I can't believe I just pulled an all-nighter with Gregory, I was thinking as I stepped off the Jeffery #6 and headed up Belmont, my ears ringing and temples pounding. I was immensely pleased with myself over last night, and yet immensely confused. This was just too much, too soon.

Had I just squandered something precious, something that would've been twice as good with Andrew? I felt like I'd lost my virginity all over again, except I hadn't felt so insecure about it the first time. What was happening here? Whom did I love?

I had to fax all of these worries out of my head, just dial 011, eight more digits, and press "start." I couldn't consider juggling feelings for Andrew and for Gregory. Maybe this head-tripping was why Andrew was so against prostitution. Maybe he had a point.

I'd overslept well past the opening of today's destination, the Gay Pride Parade.

Chicago has a lively parade boasting countless Midwesterners full of beer and pride and flaunting what they've got, and a little of what they don't. The floats are often simple, and there are always way too fucking many politicians (shades of Daddy) who would shit if their kids turned out gay but who don't mind riding into petty little offices on gay votes . . . but otherwise, the feeling of community is never so strong as it is at the big parade. In fact, that sense of community often fades into nonexistence for much of the rest of the year. But that's my fault, isn't it? Always shacked up in my room, or in my own world, or being paid to fuck men with no gay pride at all, just sexual shame. And gay money.

Joe came running up to me, looking stoned as a grunge rocker.

After the preliminaries, he exclaimed brightly, "I think this parade is going to be a turning point for me." He vogued across the pavement as easily as most of us walk, except less self-consciously. "I'm outta the house, outta the closet, and outta my head!" *Don't forget "outta your league."*

"It should be cool," I said, aloof. Joe came over and threw his arms around my shoulders.

"I can't believe you're walking up Belmont and you're not more into Gay Pride. You're a block away from a butt-load of card-carrying gay guys. Aren't you proud?"

He was so cute, so cute. His eyes were so glittery. Who decides who gets pretty eyes and who just gets eyes that see everything? I wanted to blurt out what had happened the night before, ask Joe for his take on things. Instead, I swallowed my confusion and bit my lip. "Of course," I said, "I'm proud. I like being gay. I just don't connect hedonism with politics."

"You'd make a lousy queer," Joe teased, a sort of joke against my age, his reference to the new guard when I was so removed from it, if only by a few years.

"I *invented* queer," I sneered. "What do you know from *queer?*" It was a joke, but close to the truth. Joe may have been a New Age queer, but I was out there making a queer living, radically selling my body, owning my self, an individual. Or whatever.

"I believe you invented queer. Didn't you also invent the wheel?"

He told me that he planned to trip on acid all day long, stay pretty drunk, and meet as many pretty boys as humanly possible, avoiding sleeping with any since he felt that Gay Pride Day should be reserved for partying and dancing and having fun. The fact that having sex with strangers did not top his list of fun was very telling. If it wasn't fun, why did he do it all the time?

But if he was going to stay fucked up, what if he met some guy who felt like taking advantage of him? I was constantly fretting over Joe. If only his brother Tony hadn't said I was supposed to look out for the kid.

Gloria Gaynor's voice was raised above the streets from a source up the block, where people were jammed in, watching the parade. Joe screamed, "A classic!"

He was too young to remember disco, only knew that this song was a classic because he'd been told it was.

I sometimes feel I have a morbid streak. I can't stand disco classics because I can only think of the fact that disco preceded the Plague. Of all those bodies cutting loose with abandon, partying in a single, serpentine wave of polyester and oil and sex . . . how many are dead now? If I listen to Donna Summer or Gloria Gaynor, I can only think of how fundamentalist they became, the rotten quotables attributed to them.

I have this memory of visiting a rich aunt in Miami with my parents. She was a fat, leathery old tart, as crass as an American princess gets, and drunk beyond comprehension. But we all had fun swimming in her kidney-shaped pool, strolling the beach and searching for exotic swim-life, and playing with her dog, Ruble (I still remember its name, though I had no idea what a ruble was then), the world's smartest poodle. But I can't remember the fun of that trip without thinking that now Ruble is long dead, cold in his grave. Morbid.

That's the way I saw my love life. Being in love with Andrew didn't mean my happiness, it meant Joe's misery. But at least he didn't look too miserable at the moment.

Just as Joe was preparing to leave, I realized I'd been staring at a gargantuan sore on his lip, and it dawned on me that it was a herpes sore. This shit looked fucked up, too, not like those cold sores your friend's father used to get, but more like genital herpes—not too hard to imagine how it traveled from hip to lip.

How do I know? Look, you only have to see one once to recognize them for the rest of your life.

"Joe—what's up with that thing on your lip?" So I'll never win any awards for subtlety. Joe stopped dead at my question and angrily asked me what I meant.

"Nothing—just that it looks like you should get it checked out." I was trying to sound casual. In my mind, I was calculating that Joe had told me he'd last had sex with this clubkid Max Prince about two nights previously, not at all too early for a herpes sore to sprout. Part of me was hoping he had herpes, as punishment for fucking around so irresponsibly. I shuddered when I realized I was capable of such a thought.

"I don't need to be any more hung up on my looks than I already am," he said with surprising perception. His bathroom is drowning in male cosmetics, hair-care products, lotions, tools, Kleenex . . . It was a wonder he could see how ridiculous his accoutrements were, especially considering that if he'd just taken a nap and rolled out of bed and directly onto the street, he would have ended up looking just as good, if not better.

"I'm not really worried about your *look* for the day. I'm saying that maybe you need to pop into the clinic and see if that's herpes . . ."

"*Herpes?*" An alien concept. Surely he wasn't so young he didn't remember when herpes was the most dreaded of all sexual diseases . . . I felt a cold pang of realization: *Of course* he was too young to remember when herpes was the new, big thing. *He's almost eight years younger than me.* I felt two new wrinkles wiggle out from the corners of my eyes.

"Yes, you might have herpes from, well, from any number of guys, really" (ouch!) "but most recently from Max."

From within his drunk he held firm. "I couldn't."

The conversation was over, but I envisioned Joe dancing at Boykultur's midnight-to-six rave later on, after the parade . . .

. . . Joe flailing with abandon, looking like an old man's fever dream, a juicy little Monster in rubber and boots and a dick-sock. The lights are flashing mechanically, an intricate enginelike panel of young sprockets dancing with the same precise electricity. Their desire is their lubricant; their limbs are their gears. Raves at Boykultur have a way of turning into orgies.

Joe is always the center of attention. Why not? He's extremely young and looks it, he's a natural blonde with a head full of teeth, and he has all the membership credentials for a fun date: He's got the head of hair, the pout, the beads, the biceps, the corn-fed ass, the rhythm, the inviting eyes. Except at a particularly hot rave, Joe is no hotter than the next little boy; they all look the same to their older peers who have graduated from being clubkids into being the studs who make the clubkids' hearts flutter. So Joe does what he has to to keep himself the center of attention. He smiles extra-wide. He winks. He exposes more of himself than is legal. He will give head to a man in a back room within plain sight of everyone just to stay popular . . .

Reality check: lofty thoughts from Irma La Douce here.

. . . Joe sees a guy looking at him—no major deal, except the guy has something about him that makes Joe look twice. The stranger is staring openly, gazing at Joe with an astonishing urge. He is taller than Joe, broader, with big, strong, generic arms. He is built to last, has dark, curly hair, and probably shaves his chest, which is partially exposed, a simple sterling silver cross beaming from a pierced nipple on the beginnings of an assembly-line pec. He is "swarthy." My grandmother would call him "an ethnic." Joe would call him a god.

God smiles menacingly at Joe, shaking His head to the music to emphasize how fierce He would be with Joe if given the chance. He moves His hips from his position flattened against the wall, communicating the thrusts He would use to demolish Joe, to pin him to the bed like a pretty little butterfly, caught, its wings forced apart, nailed into a monstrous child's glass display case.

Joe breaks from his friends and dances over to God and fondles His nipple-cross lasciviously. "It's nice," he says blandly. "I like it."

"I bet you do."

A half hour later, they are in God's car. It's parked beside the bar, so the ponderous rumbling of techno is heard through wall and door and metal and glass. God has Joe lick the sweat from His face, His neck. Joe is enthusiastic, excited. This guy is *sooooo* hot and *sooooo* cute . . . God is talking to Joe, telling him He wants Joe to suck Him off. Joe gets to work, mouthing God's bloated penis, suckling it like a child on its mother's breast, savoring the illicit pre-come, not even worrying about AIDS because in Canada they now say sucking is safe. As long as you don't let Him come in your mouth, which is God's next order of business, and Joe—polite— eats the semen as it jumps onto his tongue. It's automatic; a favor as a way to start out a fun new relationship.

These sorts of half-assed agreements are banal in our world. Men make them every day, defying logic, reason, intelligence, cau- tion, all for the delicious feeling of being dangerous in a world so safe, it's impossible to live in. Literally. Welcome to gay sex in the nineties.

God is ravenously horny tonight, happy to indulge Himself in a willing minor. "I gotta fuck that ass," He moans, kissing Joe furiously to help work up His organ again. Joe is assailed by an array of emotions and a confusing feeling of both the urge to allow himself to be used, and the urge to protect himself from it. In the end, Joe is too aroused by the stubby finger poking into his anus to say no. Instead, when he opens his mouth to refuse, he hears his own voice begging God to ream him out good.

It's cramped quarters in God's car, but He positions Joe over His cock and unceremoniously impales His prey, moves him up and down on His dick like it's an inanimate tool, milking it methodically. Joe feels so good, so alive. It hurts and feels good and he is aware of every minute sensation as his new lover's cock rubs in and out of his body.

"I'm gonna shoot it . . ." This time God is responsible—no sense in being *ridiculously* unsafe—and pulls the boy off of Him, jerks Himself off onto the dash of His brother's car. Joe is stroking himself, too, but will eventually give up trying to come, embar- rassed to be still trying on number one when God has blown His wad twice.

"Don't worry about me," Joe says ingratiatingly. But, of course, God will interpret this as a sign that the boy did not find

Him sexy. Not enough of a turn-on. They talk quietly, mop up, rearrange themselves, and then Joe is being driven home. He scrawls his name and number on a matchbook that will eventually be used by God's next live-in lover to light their stove top. Joe gets out of the car, comes inside, all aflutter, infatuated. *What a night! As long as I don't tell anyone, then it doesn't really count that I have just had wildly unsafe sex . . .*

I was definitely worried about my little Monster. I'd once bumped into a sleepy-faced Puerto Rican guy sneaking out of Joe's room early in the morning, and had been determined to figure out if Joe was even using a condom when he was with all these guys of his. So I waited until Joe went into the bathroom and I peeked into his room, scanning for empty packages, a box of Heavy Duties, used Kleenex, any paraphernalia that might give me a clue. Then it occurred to me that Joe would probably have deposited any sex-trash into the hall garbage, so I crept over to the alcove and started to fish around in the basket. Joe came up behind me and asked me what I was doing.

"Looking for my life—I think I may have accidentally thrown it away." He was disheveled, a defiled rag doll.

"Well, you really shouldn't dig around in the garbage." He seemed uncomfortable and slipped into his room and away from any ensuing discussion, so I decided to drop the matter.

I went back to my room and tried to keep from wondering. The next day I bought a box of a hundred anal-sex-approved condoms and two tubes of ForPlay and told both Andrew (like he'd have the need for them) and Joe that I'd been given them free at a demonstration and that they were for the household. From then on, I noticed with satisfaction as condoms disappeared, as lubricant drained away mysteriously in the night, followed by the embarrassed yet elated exits of various clubkids from Joe's chambers. He was being safe. Or, at least, *trying.*

"Monster," I coaxed sweetly, "just do me a favor and go to the clinic. I know about these things. Anyone can get herpes."

"I'll go," he said matter-of-factly, knowing he wouldn't. If he had gone to the STD clinic, I bet he would have bumped into Max there. Joe's herpes later haunted him only for the first few outbreaks. After that, and after he got over the initial heartache and feeling of self-loathing, the herpes became a mild nuisance, but also a useful reminder, a cautionary token. *It could have been worse.*

I gave up on the herpes thing, wished him fun, and hugged him gingerly, not wanting to muss his . . . *entire body.* He seemed to warm to me, and hugged me back. "Have fun, Monster," I groaned. You see, I called him "Monster" because he was anything but. He flitted up the street and into the throng of queers.

I shook off the phantoms and realized that my feelings of affection, of love, even, for Andrew, Gregory, and Joe were emerging like grass seedlings in time-lapse photography, sprouting all over the place at random. I *was* feeling proud, maybe not of being gay, just proud. Proud, good, refreshed.

I wanted to see me some parade.

I stifled a sneeze at Broadway and Belmont, and in covering my nose I noted that I hadn't shaved that morning. I stopped and felt my cheeks and chin to double-check. Nope, I really hadn't shaved. It was probably the first day I was going unshaven since my first pack of disposables at thirteen. Funny how such a little blip in your usual routine can blow your freaking mind, but it certainly did, and I wondered if it wasn't a sign of a greater, system-wide meltdown, and whether that was necessarily a bad thing.

The crowd was wild, cheering float after float, queen after queen, and even one ambidextrous, baton-twirling she-male who elicited the kinds of *oohs* and *ahs* usually reserved for a tightwire performer. S/he was fabulous, pencil-thin, bedecked in a hot pink, spangled unitard and carrying the expression of a bored society matron, as if oblivious or disdainful of the lightning baton-work of her own blurred hands.

It was warm, thank God, maybe the last warm day for some time, and the streets smelled of people, junk food, and a scent that escaped me.

I spent the parade day watching the crowd more than the floats. There were altogether too many dripping wet muscle-boys, whom I've never understood. After all, they spend all their free time conditioning their bodies to please other men's hands and *still* end up fighting with one-night stands over who gets to be fucked.

As silly as it sounds, though, it really was effecting to think that the tens (hundreds?) of thousands of screamers were almost all gay.

Gregory had refused to come with me that day, and his grinchy excuses had spooked me. He seemed very uncomfortable with the idea of the parade, and I couldn't believe he'd never in twenty years even gone to see it. It just didn't make sense.

But I was glad he'd refused, glad to be alone for a bit. I welcomed the reprieve from having to interact with people. Instead, I could observe them interacting with each other.

I didn't see a single other person I knew after Joe took off, and I wouldn't have had it any other way. A few months earlier, I'd've felt bitter and lonely at the Gay Pride Parade. But that day I felt super. I didn't need to see millions of people I knew (as some of the other spectators did) just to feel loved. I simply knew that I had Joe, Gregory, and even—though we weren't speaking—Andrew in the wings.

I staggered into my room after dusk, when the other queers were just pouring out of bars like Mother's, Dicks, or C-Street and into the bigger joints like Carol's Speakeasy, the Bistro, the rather bleakly named Vortex, or the dreaded Boykultur. I'd done enough people-watching and was feeling too pleasantly buzzed from the experience to ruin it by watching Gay Pride metamorphose into Gay Probe, with everyone who's anyone after anyone, period.

Andew was out, ironically.

I briefly worried that he'd meet a man and have a fling at the zero hour, but wiped that possibility from my head before it became entrenched. Joe was out, too, probably like a light, slumped on the floor of Boykultur, not in God's car after all.

I fed Judy, who purred like mad while she made some Tender Vittles disappear, and then I crawled into bed and checked out, feeling more comfortable with what had happened with Gregory, even if it was undeniable that Andrew was my true Renaldo.

I AM
SHOCKABLE

The night after Gay Pride Day, something unusual happened: We had a guest over to the apartment. Joe's older brother/guardian Tony was invited to hang out with us, eat pizza, watch TV, whatever. It was the first time he'd come over to the apartment for longer than an hour or so, and Joe seemed to need to see him. When Joe had mentioned the visit to me, I'd caught the sketchy depression in his eyes, the loneliness. He had a drifting relationship with his brother, the only member of his family who loved him unreservedly, despite an embarrassed unfamiliarity with the whole concept of being gay.

When I'd told Andrew that Tony was drifting over, he gave me a sheepish look and I mirrored it. Time and—for me—a lot of thinking had softened our hard silence. From Andrew's unnecessary "Thanks for warning me," I knew we were friends again . . . at least for an evening.

"Truce?" he offered.

"Truce."

I hoped we were well on our way to making up and making it.

Tony arrived around eight and we all shook

hands and got down to the business of shooting the shit, drinking beer or Evian or whatever was handy. It was amazing to see how butch we all sounded when faced with the extraordinary task of simply *talking*. Or were Andrew, Joe, and I just trying to measure up to Tony's undeniable machismo?

As we sat around, it dawned on me what a rare moment this was—we'd never all been together before. That untogetherness had incubated an unusual bond among the four of us: Joe didn't know the latest on me and Andrew, Andrew had no idea that I cared for Joe so much more than I usually let on, and Tony only knew what censored fragments Joe sometimes fed him over the phone. As for me, I have no idea what things I didn't know about. We were all intimately interrelated, but we were mostly linked via repression, hearsay, intuition, suspicion . . . very strong ties. No sarcasm.

I felt emotionally drained, so I was uncharacteristically quiet. Tony was the only guy in the room I had no sexual anxieties over, and he *was* looking pretty hot that night.

Don't worry, I don't end up fucking Tony. I'm not such a floozy after all.

Tony's sexiness was his cuteness, his sweet, innocent expressions and matter-of-fact sensuality. And his dumbness. And his straightness, let's not forget. He was drinking a Miller, looking disheveled and droopy-eyed with sleepiness. He was slouched on the big sofa next to his little brother, bad seed Joe, who was just as uncomplicated but unabashedly carnal. Joe had gotten a haircut that day, and his short blond hair was crushed in a funny way, as if he'd been sleeping on it wrong. He was in pajamas, the ratty cotton jammies (yellow with red hearts) he preferred sleeping in night after night. Together, they looked like a Bruce Weber photograph in the making: "Beef and Chicken."

Andrew was sitting cross-legged on the floor *sans* shirt, in only a pair of white Calvins like Marky Mark except with a decent face. He was the only one actually watching the dumb Stella Stevens hooker movie on TV that the rest of us pretended to watch. I sat in my chair opposite the brothers, Andrew between my knees. I scratched his back and rubbed his shoulders—I admit that under normal circumstances, I'd've been creaming doing this, but I was so mentally preoccupied, it didn't even occur to me to get a hard-on.

Tony was taking it all in stride.

It was funny to see the three roomies in various states of undress and two of us getting romantic, and there was straight ole construction dude Tony, totally suavy suave.

"She's so old to be a prostitute," Andrew remarked of the middle-aged lady on the TV in a prop boa. "How old is she? Like *fifty?*"

"More than that now," Joe said, reviving a bit with the taste of celebrity trivia and earnestly munch-slurping a bowl of Cheerios. "But maybe thirty-nine or forty when this was made—1979."

"Too old," Andrew reiterated. You did not have to be brilliant to get his point. Sensing how dumb it was to insult me when I was behind him with my hands around his neck, he shut up quick.

"I want Madonna to do a prostitute movie," Joe enthused, "A really unglamorous role, like a heroin addict or something, like *Lady Sings the Blues.*"

Tony attempted to join in. "Yeah, she'd be great at that." Joe took it as a dig, as if Tony would be snide or dumb enough to slam the Big M around the Little J.

I was just sick to be watching another prostitute movie. Why do people make so many? Why do we find prostitution so fascinating? It loses its appeal after the first transaction, then you realize what it really is: just business. There's nothing deep and meaningful, nor dark and sinister, about it, no more interesting than a grocer selling a piece of fruit.

"Hey, you guys," Tony said, "I wanna ask you three something." We all rolled our eyes in our minds, and Joe—next to Tony and so impossible for Tony to see—rolled his eyes aloud. You just *knew* it was gonna be a prelude to a barrage of completely unrelated and embarrassing questions about homosexuality. It was written—in crayon—all over his face.

"Yes?" Joe prompted, bristling.

"It's a gay thing," Tony said, "I have a question about sex that you guys can help me out with. Do you guys ever think about women having sex?"

Joe and Tony had always had mysterious little sibling run-ins about gay politics, spurred on by Tony's dullness and Joe's memory of his intense hero worship of the guy. When they quarreled, Tony would obliviously say the exact wrong things without a trace of maliciousness. Intent to hurt never counts much when someone ends up hurt anyway.

"You mean about lesbians?" I asked, cutting off Joe's attempt to jump all over the oaf.

"Not necessarily," Tony replied.

Pause.

"Well, what women have sex with other women unless they're lesbians?" Joe asked impatiently.

"Bisexual women," Tony said, proud to expose his fag-waving brother's own little unconscious prejudices. *Bravo!*

"Bisexual-schmisexual," Joe said caustically.

"That's not the point anyways—I'm asking if you ever think about women having sex, and you're not answering . . ."

"The answer, for me, is no," I said. "Don't get me wrong—it's not that I dislike women. The only thing I have against women is that men aren't more like them. I just never find myself daydreaming of rug-rubbing."

Andrew had to put his two cents in. "*I* do, Tony."

"But then you're a little . . ." Tony made a shaky hand gesture and Andrew's neck stiffened under my fingers. So Joe *had* been keeping his big brother informed on the state of affairs in our apartment.

Joe was outraged. "What an offensive thing to say! Andrew's not—" (more hand gesturing) "—he's just coming out of the closet."

"Granted, there *is* some confusion," Andrew conceded. *Tell me about it.*

"Am I being offensive?" Tony demanded, speading his arms helplessly. "I don't think so. Jesus, Joe, every move I make is offensive to you. Every time I have a question, you get pissed off."

"No, Tony, no," Joe spoke over him, "I don't think about women having sex. Why would I? Why would you ask that? You just wish I'd think—"

"Oh, here we go! Here we go! I'm the hetero, I'm the bad guy. Tell him—tell him I'm no bigot." Odd that he'd turn to me, though I did, in fact, agree.

"Why don't you just tell us why you're asking us this thing about women?" I suggested peevishly, more interested in pushing buttons than moderating.

Tony told us his bi girlfriend mostly liked women and yet fantasized about gay guys having sex. This intrigued us all and we sat for a moment digesting it. This guy put up with a *bi* girlfriend?

"Gee—she sounds more—" (shaky hand gesture) "—than *me*," Andrew joked.

"Closet hetero," Joe decreed.

"I think it makes sense that she'd have that fantasy," I said, "for what it's worth. It's like straight men fantasizing about lesbians . . . sort of."

"Me, I don't get it," Tony said. "And I mean—it's like, she likes women more than me and now she's got a thing for gay guys—she likes *everybody* more than me."

"Then maybe it says something about you that you stay with her," Joe said.

Tony surprised us all by pulling his brother over to him and bear-hugging him. Joe kicked his feet in the air comically while Tony kissed his face mockingly. "Maybe it says something about me that I hang out with three fags."

Joe, almost won over, suddenly struggled away, half-amused, half-annoyed. He hated the word "fag" even when fags used it, but hearing Tony say it struck a nerve. "Don't use that word for me," he scolded. "Don't say it to me. I don't need you calling me a fag—I get called 'fag' enough already. It's an ugly word—it makes me feel like shit."

Tony always took his brother's irrational tirades to heart. He pulled Joe back to him and cradled him like a baby—the jammies really helped the image. Joe relaxed and you could see how much they loved each other. It was sweet to see big, macho Tony so tender. Then he shocked the hell out of us all.

Caressing Joe like a baby, Tony leaned down and kissed his brother on the lips. It was chaste, yet not brotherly. More motherly, but with an unmistakably (shaky hand gesture) element to it. I think Andrew was disgusted—he tensed up and we never discussed the incident later. I was in disbelief—but I masturbate over it to this day. I know, I know, *What's up with all this incest all over the place?* Search me. Maybe since I only have sisters, it doesn't gross me out as much.

Tony looked down at a stunned Joe and said, "So now I'm a fag, too, OK?"

We knew he wasn't really, but the gesture was quite sincere.

We killed the hooker movie and Andrew and I retired to our rooms, awkwardly silent as the two brothers talked into the wee hours.

I AM
GULLIBLE

The rest of my life may have been sketchy, but one thing was for sure: I couldn't sleep with Gregory again. Andrew was against my dates, and though the jury was still out on whether I'd give them up, I had to admit that Gregory was more than a "date" to me. He'd become too important to me; seeing him would be an undeniable betrayal of Andrew. I couldn't love Andrew while simultaneously cultivating a loving relationship with Gregory. That was why I'd freaked— I'd known my relationship with Gregory had to change drastically the moment we'd gotten intimate. It had to change, or it had to end.

I had always thought the worst day of my life was the day Cousin Andy rejected me. Typically, that was overdramatization. Before Andy and I had sex, I feared that if he knew how I felt about him, he would be unreceptive. When he was, even after we did it, it was disastrous simply because it was a playing out of my worst fears.

The real worst day of my life was ten times worse because I never even saw it coming. It was like the freaky nightmare that turns normally effervescent kids into paralytic zombies, crawling wordlessly into their parents' beds.

It was Gregory. I know you think that I found Gregory dead or something. Every story with a charming old man in it ends in a heart-tugging funeral. Truthfully, I did often worry not only that Gregory would die on me, but that I'd be the one to find him, curled up and frigid, hours gone. I only *wish*.

I was due to meet Gregory at his place later in the evening, but I decided to drop by early to surprise him.

I was suffocating. The elevator was slower than ever, full beyond capacity with students.

As students piled off, one figure was left slumping in the corner of the lift, one pudgy old man with a mane of white hair and a severe set of laugh lines, except probably they weren't caused by laughing since he seemed the most humorless goat in the world. I studied him openly, comparing him to Gregory, having a hard time reconciling this repulsive beast with the cute old bird I'd recently screwed. This guy was at most Gregory's age, but he certainly wore it badly. He also wore a wickedly heavy-looking black trench coat that he'd obviously purchased on VE-day, or possibly to celebrate the end of the Civil War. *There, but for the taste of God, go I.*

The man was looking back at me and I smiled curtly. It must have made me look open to conversation, for he grumped about the slowness of the elevator and made a to-do about examining his watch.

"It's always *slow* when I am *late*."

I nodded. We approached the top floor, and I suddenly realized this old guy was going there, too. Who could he be going to see but Gregory? Or was he a neighboring student's grandfather?

I acted like I was being concerned for him, and offered to punch a button on the panel—"Oh, are you going to the top, too?"

He looked offended and said that yes he was, was I?

I nodded, perplexed. "Are you a friend of Gregory's?" I queried indiscreetly. If the guy was, I'd pretend I was a student, not going to visit Gregory at all.

"Yes. Do you know Gregory?" he asked, eyebrows arched,

condescension heavy in his accented voice. He sounded European, and from the yellow fringe at the nape of his neck, I could see his hair had once been black. His eyes were dead in their sockets, muddied and sunken, deep and dark like burned-out lightbulbs, but still seeing, almost a century after they first saw.

"Neighbors." I shrugged mock-cheerfully. "Are you his brother?" I asked, a question a neighbor kid might ask one old man visiting another.

"No," he said tentatively. "But he was the friend of my brother's."

I felt a sudden inkling of disaster. The doors purred and opened and the man nodded at me and shambled off toward Gregory's apartment, a little befuddled that I did not get off after all. I stayed on the elevator and rode it all the way back down, got off and slumped onto a bench inside the lobby, waiting.

There was only one person this man could be, despite the possibility that he could be *anybody*. I had the strongest sense of coincidence—this *had* to be Renaldo's brother. Funny, from Gregory's brief description, I'd envisioned Renaldo's brother to be a shut-in. This guy was decrepit but mobile.

I had never doubted Gregory in any way, so I jumped at the chance.

My mind chided my humanity for having believed anything anybody ever said. Still, this was all premature. That man could—realistically—be Moses before being Renaldo's brother.

I sat very still on the bench, aware that a lot of kids were streaking past me in every direction, though I didn't pay attention to anyone. I had even stopped thinking about Gregory and the Mystery Man; I was vegetating, not letting myself play out the scenario before it occurred.

I don't know how long it took, but at some point the old man was rustling past me, looking pleased with his little visit, much sunnier than when he'd arrived, and I stood up to get the door for him. He murmured a thank you, then noticed I was the same guy from the elevator and nodded familiarly, a little disoriented.

"Did you have a nice time?" I asked.

"Yes," he said meekly, "Thank you."

"Are you Renaldo's brother?" I asked in a similarly chitchatty tone. My face was numb and my heart zigzagged in my chest. It was not often that I was so direct, at least with strangers, whom I usually felt compelled to charm.

The old man looked shocked, then smiled in a very small, bittersweet way, heartbreaking to see on the face of such a tough old rusted nail. "Why, yes, yes I am. I am Carlo—but you could not have known my brother . . . He's been gone . . . *years . . .*" He gestured broadly, a sweep of the hand that encompassed my entire life and the least significant, latter portion of his.

"No," I said, "but Gregory loved him very much." This was inappropriately received with a look of discomfort and surprise; not at all what I'd anticipated—oh, God. "He's told me all about him . . ."

"You must be very close to Gregory for him to have told you about his schoolboy crushes," the man chuckled nervously, secretively, glancing about to check for ears. Then, "Good-bye." He attempted to shuffle away.

I persisted. "But they were lovers," I stated plainly, "right?" *Please—I need this to be the truth.*

The old man looked disturbed. "No," he said firmly, convincingly. "Not at all. Who told you that? Did Gregory tell you that?"

I said yes.

Carlo's expression drifted from anger and alarm to that put-upon look that people get when dealing with a dotty grandmother or hopelessly retarded child. Gregory.

We staked out a corner near the door and the man explained everything succinctly, destroyed me completely with the efficiency and goodwill of a surgeon.

"Gregory is a dear, dear man," he began, "but a lonely man. And, sometimes, a cruel man. Cruel because he is so *needy.* He loved my brother from the time they were young men working as bellhops here in the thirties. He was actually my brother's best friend for years before I met him. We became close, but it took another quarter of a century before Gregory was able to say aloud to me that he was a homosexual, despite the fact that *I* had been very open to *him* from the beginning, despite the fact that I knew from the moment I met him that he was in love with my brother." Carlo was spilling his guts with great, theatrical animation, as if he'd been dying to tell someone his theories on the subject for ages. So Carlo was gay, too, a fact that had escaped me earlier—no tell-tale signs in one so old and austere. As a youth, he may have been ridiculously gorgeous, flaming, impulsive, macho, anything . . . My mind tried to wander from the horror that he was telling me.

"Gregory was a tormented man then, satisfied to be uselessly in love with a heterosexual who would never love him back, one who would also never realize there was romance in Gregory's heart in the first place so could never reject him as a lover. It makes no sense today, with everyone so open, so full of *pride*, really. It made no sense to me *then*, either, even when *everybody*, even queers, thought queers were beneath contempt. Gregory came out in the sixties, in his fifties. He was never my brother's lover because my brother loved only women, and because my brother was dead before Gregory came out to a single soul. Gregory hasn't had any 'lovers,' really . . ."

I was devastated, but I did not miss the intimation. I could not think—do I protest that I am *not* Gregory's lover, affirm that I *am* Gregory's lover, pretend not to catch his implied question? Was I Gregory's lover? *Gregory hasn't had any lovers, really* . . . It was that "really" that crucified. *Really.* I was not Gregory's lover; not *really*.

Gregory was one of my first friends, a sort of role model for how I saw myself as an old queer. He was the first client I'd ever had any feelings for, and now I was faced with the fact that our relationship was, to him, just a big lie. I'd never do that to anyone, lead him on like that. I felt so hurt that I had to consider . . . Gregory was a first friend, and may have been even more.

"He pays me," I said abruptly, closing the other man's mouth. I was blinking furiously. With three words, I canceled my emotional relationship with Gregory. It's called saving face, even if the junk behind your face is feeling pretty fucked up.

Carlo frowned a bit and then forced a polite smile. "At any rate," he clucked, "that is neither *here*, nor *there*. I just thought you should know that Gregory is a dear, dear man . . . who can not be trusted to tell the truth." Carlo gathered himself into his ancient coat and continued out the door and into the sunny courtyard out front.

I was immersed in pity for Gregory, contempt for my own gullibility. Embarrassment so deep, it scalded away the immediate pain. One of those moments when one feels an inch high, except I felt smaller still, nonexistent. My entire friendship with Gregory was nonexistent, predicated on a self-serving, self-loathing lie, perhaps a lie fabricated just to play out a sex game. But that was fair, wasn't it? Wasn't that what was supposed to happen in the first place? Oh, to have had nothing but a quick blow job with Master Gregory, instead of this rich antic.

Then there was the pathos. Gregory was . . . a failure. A complete and utter wreck of a man, impotent. I'd almost admired him. Had loved him. But he was as pitiful as the rest; worse. And I was worse still, for believing.

I left.

I never saw Gregory again, but he is still alive. He calls from time to time, but always gets the hint when I make excuses to get off the phone, to avoid meeting with him. I suspect he figured out that I had figured him out. Maybe Carlo said something. Scolded him.

I knew I could never see Gregory again because if I did, I would either die of shame or break his neck. I'd learned a lot from him, some of which I don't think anyone should ever have to learn.

And you wonder why I have a hard time getting close to people.

CONFESSION
REDUX

Have I ever fallen in love?
Yes. Twice.

I AM A CRY-BABY

After busing back to the North Side, I went for a walk. Whenever something crushes me, I walk, like a feisty roach after a rain of dead-on swats.

Gregory's masquerade hanging over me like a cloud of insecticide, I walked up my street, lost in thought. I just kept replaying an ugly scene in my head, a brief exchange I'd once had with Gregory: "My youngest friends," Gregory had sighed dryly, "forty years—*fifty* years my junior, all died. All my old friends are dead and I'm simply too tired to make more just now." I had winced at the prospect. "You're it. You're it."

It's scary—people who reinvent their histories. Who knows who's for real? Most people are insignificant enough that they are automatically taken at their word. What if they decide to just make things up? Make themselves up? I can say that my confessions are all real, but why should you believe me? Maybe I am my own best creation, a walking novel. The nothing life.

Halsted was a big scene that day, full of tanned clones and various unexciting individualistic second-glancers, suddenly demonstrative straight couples, and the KFC-eating black drag queens who'd never hesitate to offer histrionic critiques of your nerdy Gap-wear even though their own ensembles often consisted of stretched-out children's T-shirts with cartoon characters on them. It was unbearably sunny, overhot. Indian summer.

I walked blindly toward the lake, walking until I had to either stop or get wet. I settled on my favorite outcropping at the Rocks, alien-looking manmade embankments at the edge of Lake Michigan that serve to keep the water in its place and also provide a festive cruising ground for the locals.

Cruising has made me think of an afternoon I once spent in the tiny park in front of my dorm, watching people enjoying a sunny BBQ day. There was this little rug rat whose parents were pretty much absorbed in a minor argument, and he was trying to make friends with two other little boys who were having an excellent time pretending to kill each other. The rug rat hovered around the periphery of the other boys' play circle, sort of revving up, looking at them expectantly, trying to seem like an attractive playmate. Finally one of the other boys called out, "What you want?" and the rug rat said with a shrug, "I just wanna play," and the first boy made a funny show of seeming put-upon, then said, "Well, c'mon." The rug rat smiled and hopped into their midst, and the trio started an elaborate game of warfare without skipping a beat.

That moment was the essence of cruising. The cruisers are just little boys who want to be accepted, who want to play. Gay guys are just little boys trying to make our way in adult bodies, except so many rules have changed in the adult world that it's hard to know how to act, what's appropriate to say or do. More often than not, we offend one another in invisible ways that end up destroying our budding friendships, despite the fact that neither friend realizes exactly *why.*

We're boys inside, some of us, stunted, hung up on the simpler times when, as adolescents, we were so close to our needs. Why do you think there are so many minors having sex in this story? Because Allen Ginsberg is ghosting it? No, because sex is more than just airborne jism, and because adolescence is the time when we have all the most important sex. Until much, much later, when another not-just-sexual encounter jars you awake and you become a mature man. Some never have that encounter, and wind up laughably acting fifteen at fifty. Lucky me, I was about to even out at twenty-five.

I was baking on the outside, but already boiled to nothing inside. Gregory had been so fucking callous, so callous fucking. I may have been using him in a way, but I had always been up front about my intentions. I'd never lied to him. He had done nothing *but* lie to me. Everyone lies, but you only lie about certain things to certain people. You don't lie about everything to a person. Unless, of course, it's a person of no consequence.

There was a reasonably handsome guy sitting near me; had been there before I sat down. Now it appeared that he thought my arrival had been an overture—he scooted over closer to me, smiled disarmingly, gestured to the lake.

"Pretty amazing, isn't it?" he offered. Handsome was about thirty, had short, thick, dark hair, a cheesily appealing little mustache (*Chicago is the capital of facial hair*), nice shoulders, a dimple, and laugh lines. He was Errol Flynnish, except hopelessly midwestern, domesticated. He was sweet.

In one instant, I was looking at the perfectly still lake, at the breathtaking blue and stabbing sparkles that filled my vision, then I was looking at Handsome, then I was lost. I don't remember starting to cry, or feeling my eyes well up, or feeling anything. I just suddenly found myself bawling my eyes out in loud, convulsive heaves. My face streamed with tears, the muscles slack with despair. Handsome had scooched up beside me and taken me into his arms gingerly, nervously, perhaps having first looked around to see if anyone was watching the crazy boy cry. He was soothing just by being there, just for having strong arms. He had built those arms in a gym; they were too full and the muscles too firm to be God-given. I regretted ever begrudging the muscle-boys their obsessive habits; here was a very good reason to have killer biceps.

Gay muscles are more than just currency after all. Handsome's musculature may have been synthetic, but his eyes were the eyes of a natural man.

I gradually ran out of tears, but let myself stay helpless in his arms. My face was against his chest, my cheek touching his bare, furry skin where it disappeared into a white tank top. I could smell the sweat on his chest, and I concentrated on that fragrance, analyzing it a thousand ways, comparing it in my mind to the smell of Andrew, to the smell of Gregory, to the smell of other men. I just kept *thinking* as hard as I could to offset the fact that I was pretty lost in *feeling*.

"I'm okay," I said, sitting back up, drawing my knees to my chest and locking my arms around them. I didn't bother trying to conceal my eyes—we were too close for the red to seem anything but red. Handsome was genuinely concerned, but also attracted, for lack of any other available quarry. Don't forget that I was sitting in a prime cruising locale. I knew I had to get out of there before he sullied his compassion with a pass.

He tried to lighten the moment. "You sure are an emotional guy." He grinned.

"Yes," I said, smiling, "I am." I stood up and apologized, which he waved away, and then told him I had to get going. "Enjoy the lake." I took off.

I know it's sentimental fluff, but it really happened that way. And it was too important to alter, to make edgier or funnier. Andrew was right: Not everything is about "ha." Some things are about "Aha!"

I AM
FLEXIBLE

Defeat.

It had been over a week since Andrew and I had had it out over my prostitution, days spent avoiding each other before the shaky truce when Tony visited. I had Gregory to wipe from my mind, clients to please, Joe to fret over. But I did love Andrew—love exploding uncontrollably all over everyone near me—and when he asked me out on a conciliatory date, I was touched and jumped at the opportunity.

He'd caught me early in the morning. I was groggy, lurching around my room, feeling hung over (on what? Evian?). Andrew poked his head in and said, "G'morning."

I responded, then drew back, having forgotten the tension for a second.

"Look," he said. Isn't it funny how people will start out with a command to "look" when they're about to be sincere? It's like they're saying, "See? No tricks up my sleeve. I'm being for real here."

"Look, can we do something tonight?"

"Like what?"

He came into my room a little more, encouraged. "Like . . . I don't know . . . a movie? Eating, drinking . . ."

"Talking?"

"Talking."

I was easy that day. "Yeah. Let's."

We'd eaten at an old standby—Rose's—savoring shrimp pasta and popcorn squid and squinting at each other in faintest candlelight. Then, on impulse, we cabbed to the Water Tower complex on Michigan Avenue.

It was black as pitch that night, but the bridge was as bright as high noon, lit by the strange glass kliegs that line the riverbanks and blind you if you stare at them.

I stared until I could only see red and had to lean against Andrew rather than topple over into the icy water.

There was a stream of evening traffic, but no other pedestrians. We didn't say a word; we didn't need to. We were back in love.

As we returned from our first night out alone together, I could practically *hear* the wheels turning in Andrew's head. He was definitely not whipped yet, and was hard at work trying to come up with a way to convince me to stop being me. *Good luck,* I thought, and I meant it.

I was more in the mood for a nonconfrontational evening.

We'd left Judy with Joe. Her sneezing had turned into kitty flu, and Andrew had been certain she wouldn't die *only* if she was being watched.

We knocked on Joe's door and it cracked open. Joe squinted out at us from within.

"Oh . . . you're back . . ." He opened up and let us in. His room was ten times warmer than it needed to be. The fake fire had probably been raging all evening. As I passed Joe, I studied his face and found him much more attractive like this, rumpled and unsmiling. He smelled better unclean, too, after a few hours in bed in his infernolike apartment.

"How went it?" he asked, still sleepy-eyed but bopping to the kitchen to locate some OJ in the fridge. I was amused to discover that he was wearing white long underwear with a little door in the seat.

"Where's Judy?" I asked, searching for but not detecting her tiny furry form.

"She's in my bed." Joe grinned. "She fell asleep on my pillow, so I went without."

We all plopped down next to each other on the floor.

"OJ?" Joe offered. Andrew and I turned him down and we fell silent. I grew uncomfortable sitting there, all so physically and emotionally close, enmeshed practically. It was like the atmosphere at my first prospective three-way, the instant before one of the women had laughingly suggested we all get naked. Both of the women had done just that, and I had had to say good-bye.

I had no realistic fear that anything like *that* was about to happen, but then maybe that sort of event would have been preferable to the current one. After all, I had gotten up and left my first shot at a three-way, but this one was a little more complex, subtler, and just about impossible to step out of gracefully.

I was staring fully into Joe's eyes, pale blue irises protected by naturally elegant lashes, eyes now unsuccessfully trying to dodge my gaze. He gave in and stared back, questioningly. I couldn't come out and say, *Joe, I know you want me, you know a part of me wants you, but it'll never work out and oh-by-the-way, I am about to finally get nailed by Andrew.* Nothing could be stated within this triangle, at least not with all three of us present. So I stared at Joe, and felt my eyes telling the story I simply could not tell in puns, innuendos, *words*.

I detected Andrew watching us, looking mostly at me. Andrew was equidistant from me and Joe, yet his physical presence weighed so much more heavily toward me, I was sure Joe could feel it. In an instant, Joe's eyes guessed the turn of events.

"There's this guy who was in the building today . . ." Joe started, imbuing as much excitement in his voice as possible. He'd met a *gorgeous* Italian student, Mauro, a friend of that insufferable old beast downstairs. Mauro was slim to the point of being skinny, with a big smile and jet-black curls. To hear Joe describe him, he was Mr. Right, all after a fifteen-minute conversation that had resulted in an exchange of numbers.

"That's cool, Joe." Andrew had bought the whole story. Not

that I suspected Joe was lying—he eventually did go out briefly with Mauro, whom we later nicknamed "Hair-Man" because of what Joe reported to be a pelt of fur under Mauro's innocent-looking shirt. I knew there really had been a Mauro. But Joe's enthusiasm was a facade. We all knew who he really wanted. *Oh, well. There are plenty of other me's to be had.* Or are there?

I scooped up Judy on the way out, and Andrew and I left Joe in the smoldering darkness.

"Good night, you two."

I was charged with anticipation wondering if we were going to do it this night after all the torture. The whole question of my activities remained unanswered. I had not promised to stop, and he hadn't said he could accept me as is. Since there *was* the possibility we were about to sleep together, I was fighting a fear I hadn't had time to entertain until now . . . *What if I'm too good?* I had been having sex constantly for years and was now practiced enough to get a man coming as quickly and intensely as possible. What if Andrew found me too . . . *professional?* What if I enjoyed the sex thoroughly, but he came away unsatisfied, yearning for some sort of "romance" I couldn't give him? The only thing worse than making a pass at someone and getting turned down is actually having your version of great sex with him and realizing he didn't like it.

I boldly crawled into Andrew's bed while he was in the shower, wanting to jerk off as usual whenever he hit the water, but restraining myself. I was fully clothed to be less of an initial threat. But if I didn't get it tonight, Andrew wouldn't live to see tomorrow.

He strolled into his bedroom completely naked, glistening with water and dragging a towel across his face before realizing I was sitting there, my eyes absorbing every wet inch of his body.

Andrew dropped the towel and looked at me drop-jawed, then narrowed his gaze and grinned. Uh-oh, he'd just figured something out: his strategy for getting me to give up prostitution.

"What are you thinking?" I prompted, my legs rubbing together under the covers to keep warm.

I envisioned the jacket of a classic bodice-ripper romance, my large breasts spilling over my corset as the virile Andrew with his Fabio mane drew me into him for the kill. The next image I conjured up was considerably more romantic. I saw Andrew kissing me warmly, stroking my cheek. Jesus! We hadn't even really *kissed* yet, not with tongues, lips, teeth, and gums.

"I'm thinking about you," he said, slipping under the covers next to me, nuzzling me affectionately. I was only too eager to respond, but then he halted what I'd thought imminent and whispered: "But first, you have one last chance to tell me why you're a prostitute. *Really.*"

I stiffened, claustrophobic being so near him, even though nearness was all I'd ever craved from Andrew.

"I don't know," I replied quickly.

His hand came to rest under my shirt on my bare belly, then moved in slow, caressing circles as he coaxed me verbally. "Come on," he breathed, "you have to have an *idea* . . . Try telling me what you *like* about it."

Nothing. Everything.

I liked the money. I liked the leisure. I liked making men feel good for ten minutes, even if I felt crummy that day. I liked the control. I liked the attention. I liked being desirable.

I hated the times when they "fell in love" with me. I hated seeing pictures of wives. I hated the fear of sexual diseases. I hated being depressed and still having to fuck. I hated doing my taxes. I hated being fooled by Gregory.

Most of all, I hated *questions.*

"I like the money," I offered, my stock answer to everything. "And so do you—without it, you'd be paying another hundred or two a month."

He smiled and bit back any sort of angry retort, if he'd had one.

"You are a genius. You could make more money at a desk job."

I was physically succumbing to the belly massage, but mentally still defensive enough to keep fighting him. "I don't *do* desk jobs."

He pulled himself up on top of me, resting on his elbows at either side of me, staring down directly into my eyes, shower-water dripping onto my eyelids, nose, lips. Then he became smug.

"OK, then. If you like the money so much, I'll pay you," he said.

My face flashed disgust and I immediately regretted it, because I knew he had seen it and would use it against me.

"You see?" He smiled. "It would bother you if *I* paid you, but your main reason for having sex with your . . . dates . . . is for money, so you must have more respect for me than you do for them, and if you respect me, you'll—"

"That's not true. It wouldn't bother me if you paid me. In fact, I *insist* that you do. Every time."

"That's fair. But there is one difference between me and them. You'd still be expected to give me pleasure, but you'd actually be able to get a *lot* of pleasure yourself. So give me a reduced rate. I'll drop a penny in a jar every time I make love to you. How's that?"

Talk about wage cuts! What an insult.

"Why the sudden change?" I asked.

"Sudden change?" he said. "What's sudden? It's taken me a year to even think this up. The change is on *your* part." Still teasing.

I wriggled under him in protest, but stopped dead when I felt how hard he was. *God, it's big* . . . It's not superbig, but when a guy has his hard-on pressed against you, it's hard not to think *God, it's big* . . . I grew weak with submission and my sex antennae, ancient but still functional, did handstands.

"You're not going anywhere, little boy. And you don't fool me one bit." And then he kissed me.

I felt his tongue before his lips and was immediately drawn into the fray. My clothes were especially resistant to removal that day, but as soon as every shred of cloth hit the floor (except for the socks . . . ya *gotta* love keeping your socks on), I felt like a little kid with an ice cream sundae . . . a banana split, even. Skin never feels so good as when it's rubbing against more skin, and Andrew's postshower dew tasted like his famous musk always smelled. It was incredible, mind-bending sex charged with a year of pursuit and my thrill at for once shutting up and letting someone dominate me completely.

After, he was kissing me again, my legs draped over his shoulders and both of us more wet than dry. My sanctimonious sphincter was no more, rudely invaded and abused for another's pleasure, in the process freeing it from its reluctant dormancy. While he fucked me, I'd kept thinking (among many, many other things) that for a puritanical boy with hang-ups about prostitution, Andrew did me like a madman, almost like he'd planned it all along.

But of course, he hadn't. Any more than I had. *He* may have seen it coming, *I* may have seen it coming, but neither of us knew for sure it would *really* happen until we were in the middle of it.

It was deliciously unsafe, easily the most dangerous sex of my life. The risks were incalculable, especially for him, and the danger of AIDS a potent symbol of all the deeper risks in consummating this particular affair.

Sometimes you instinctively decide to take risks that common sense says you shouldn't. I'll let you know if that one returns to haunt me.

But at the time, all I knew was that I could smell flowers burning.

While we showered, Andrew wouldn't let go of me. He just held me strongly and whispered, "I love you so much, X."

Of course, I won't go into raunchier detail about my first encounter with Andrew. Some moments are better left unshared. Look how sucky "Moonlighting" got. So just imagine.

I was able, with much of Andrew's support, to make the dozen or so phone calls necessary to post my retirement. Andrew never knew it, but I *did* have the decency to give the judge two weeks' notice.

In my bliss, in my stupor of radical newness at the prospect of basically leaving prostitution to become the lover of a sidewardly mobile Blockbuster Video manager, I knew I would spend the rest of my life with Andrew. He would become the steadiest customer of my life, never neglecting to pay me for a service. Those pennies would outgrow their jar and we would start slipping them into bank-issue rolls to conserve space. I would put Judy through college on pennies.

I also believed I'd never hustle again.

Don't you believe *it.*

I AM
DESPERATE

Twenty-three confessions, one for each year of my life up till I got together with Andrew, barring those last two years at the U of C when I was too busy studying to be doing anything worth confessing.

If I've left anything out, it's probably on purpose. You can't expect to know *everything*. You never get to hear *everything* in a confession, only what the sinner feels he *must* tell.

Andrew and I moved to a one-bedroom off Belmont, still in Boy's Town but no cohabiting with Joe, who took a place with his brother. We see those two all the time now that Tony's "out." Don't be cross with me—for once, I had *no* idea, even after their weird kiss, which I still don't believe was what you think it was. Regardless, my sex antennae must've been out to lunch. Tony and Joe both have lovers now, too . . . *also* brothers. Beginner's luck.

I love Andrew and I don't doubt I'll be with him for the long haul. He still makes my knees knock and my heart thud, even when he brings up all the old arguments about hooking.

Lest you lose respect for my stubborn will, I *did* eventually return to my calling . . . sort of. I still turn the occasional trick here and there (Norman the pediatrician, the forever judge, a few others), and I've yet to hold down a real job.

Let me explain.

I have a monstrous savings account and absolutely no remorse over how I earned it. This world is too nasty to spend time feeling guilty over how you're surviving in it. Instead of clerking or flipping burgers or owning my own boutique, pumping gas or selling drugs or becoming a doctor, I made an early bundle in the skin trade. *Yawn.*

Now I make a little pocket money as a storyteller (not a "writer"—*I hate that word!*). I sell to lit mags, anthologies, lots of porno rags. But I make much more money by actually visiting men and reading them my erotic tales, which boils down to dirty talking with a script. It's totally new, an innovation on the world's oldest profession. Joe once accused me of having invented the wheel, and he wasn't far off—I *re*invented it. If I don't have sex with the men and still get the same money, why bother mussing my hair, right?

I'll be selling these confessions to whatever offers me the most money. Maybe a magazine, or a legit publisher, or maybe Mr. Johnny Depp will option my story for one hundred thousand fast, easy bucks.

Once a whore, always a whore.

Can life go on like this? Course not. Something will have to give, even if that something is the eventual depletion of my savings. Let's face it—there aren't as many guys out there who're willing to toss around three to four figures for what I like to call "verbal sex." I'll eventually lose my regular customers, and I expect it'll be difficult to locate more. But there's no sense in not doing what I want to do now simply because I may not be able to do what I want to do later. That's like not being beautiful when you're young simply because you won't necessarily be beautiful when you're old. Or refusing to love simply because you may reach a point when you are incapable of loving anymore.

I'm all for the here and now. And right now, I'm enjoying telling stories like Gregory used to. And who'll be hurt if I lie a little? Or a lot? After all, I'm a *man* who can fake orgasm convincingly. Why waste such talent on telling the boring truth all the time?

All I'm doing now is living and loving, which is more than I can say for most people. Which is more than I can say for myself before the events of these confessions.

Now, if you'll excuse me, my pediatrician is big on punctuality.

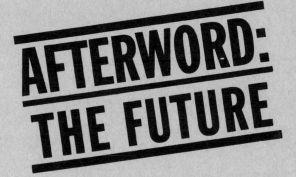

So how many Hail Marys is that?

SEXUAL
INDEX

back-room sex: 141
body licking/kissing: 67, 91, 92, 124, 135, 142

cherry-bombing (virginity, loss of): 18, 26, 27,
    36–46, 56, 63–69, 78, 80, 122
confusion, sexual: 19, 32, 34, 45–47, 55–56, 62,
    70–73, 75, 97–99, 102, 112–113, 116, 120,
    149–151
crush: 14

"Daddy"/"boy" scene: 7–10
dating: 3, 14
dirty talk: 68, 76
doggie bag fever (fetish for uncircumcised/"uncut"
    penises): 34, 67
dry humping: 9

exhibitionism: 16, 20–22, 23–24, 59–60, 91–92, 93,
    141

foot fetish: 31, 115

gang-banging (let's reclaim that term for orgies, shall
    we?): 82, 131, 141

heterosexual intercourse: 56, 126, 131, 134
homosexuality, male: throughout
Hulk Hogan fever (fetish for wrestling/roughhousing): 33

incest: 38–46, 58, 129, 132–133, 151

jungle fever (fetish for another race): 30

kissing: 23, 43, 66–67, 68, 92, 103, 105, 110, 132, 134–135,
 150, 167, 168, 169, 171

leg fetish: 22, 124
lust: throughout

making a mini Jackson Pollack (male orgasm): 4, 37, 44, 68,
 74–75, 79, 93, 129, 136, 142, 160, 172
making a pit stop (underarm fetish): 9, 92
milking the monkey (male masturbation): 4, 37, 55–56, 67, 71,
 74–75, 79, 93, 129, 133, 166

packing the groceries (anal sex): (acknowledgments), 9, 36–46,
 56, 63–69, 76, 82, 91, 93, 95, 105, 116, 121, 124, 135–136,
 142, 143, 144, 169
pedophilia: 7–8, 10
potluck (sexual versatility): 38
promiscuity: 25, 51, 94, 98, 124–125
prostitution: throughout
pucker-surfing (analingus/"rimming"): 37, 79, 92–93, 95

rest-area sex: 96
risky sex: throughout
rough sex: 9, 30, 63
rug-rubbing (lesbianism): (acknowledgments), 56, 149

seduction: 20–22, 23–24, 27–28
shetland fever (hair fetish): 22, 30, 165
smell fetish: 28, 67, 83, 162, 168

MATTHEW RETTENMUND

sock fetish: 71, 92, 168
staring/eye contact: 13–14, 16, 64–65, 129
Stipe-ulation (bisexuality): 85, 98, 149, 150
sweat fetish: 3, 67, 77, 162
sweatpants fetish: 9
sympathy fuck: 22, 105

taking Bruce's temperature (digital sex/"finger-fucking"): 9, 37, 68, 131, 142
teatillation (nipple stimulation): 67, 74, 135, 141
tickling fetish ("being ho-ho-horny"): 54
tickling the Ivory (clean fetish): 28, 91–92, 166
tonsil-tuning (male-to-male oral sex/"blow jobs"): 38, 48, 55, 67–68, 78, 79, 91, 92, 94, 95, 124, 126, 135, 141, 142, 157

underwear fetish: 70, 104, 115, 130, 147

verbal sex™: 3, 172
voyeurism: 22, 60, 93